# Metaphorosis

---

## April 2021

---

Beautifully made speculative fiction

# Also from Metaphorosis

## Verdage

*Reading 5X5 x2: Duets*
*Score – an SFF symphony*
*Reading 5X5: Readers' Edition*
*Reading 5X5: Writers' Edition*

## Metaphorosis Magazine

*Metaphorosis: Best of 20xx*
*Metaphorosis 20xx: The Complete Stories*
*annual issues, from 2016*
*Monthly issues*

## Plant Based Press

*Best Vegan Science Fiction & Fantasy*
*annual issues, from 2016*

## Vestige

*Tower of Mud and Straw*
by Yaroslav Barsukov

## from B. Morris Allen

*Susurrus*
*Allenthology: Volume I*
*Tocsin: and other stories*
*Start with Stones: collected stories*
*Metaphorosis: a collection of stories*

# Metaphorosis

*April 2021*

edited by
B. Morris Allen

ISSN: 2573-136X (online)
ISBN: 978-1-64076-197-1 (e-book)
ISBN: 978-1-64076-198-8 (paperback)

Metaphorosis
a magazine of speculative fiction
from
Metaphorosis Publishing

Neskowin

# April 2021

# The Big S

David Hammond

It was another New Year's Eve at my brother-in-law's house on the lake. Aunt Margaret sent me to the kitchen to retrieve the chocolate-covered strawberries, her eyes glassy and cheeks flushed from champagne.

The kitchen lights were off, but moonlight from the window illuminated the tray of strawberries on the countertop. By the sink, a chef's knife lay across an unwashed cutting board. I was about to rinse them off and put them in the drying rack, but I was struck by the reflection of icy blue moonlight on the blade. I leaned down for a closer look. The cutting board was slightly damp. It smelled of onions.

Perspiration broke out on my forehead. I teetered momentarily and steadied myself with a hand on the counter. Had I drunk too much champagne myself? After delivering the strawberries to the stuffy living room, I stepped outside to cool off.

Pipe smoke wafted from a corner of the porch. I couldn't identify the man's face in the shadow of an overhanging pine but recognized the plaid shirt, rumpled jeans, and thin hands of my brother-in-law's uncle, Tim.

"Hi, Tim."

Tim tapped his pipe on his knee. "Hi, Glen." He leaned forward to rest his elbows on his knees, and as his face moved out of the shadow of the pine, moonlight glistened on his wet cheeks.

He had been weeping.

So what? Aunt Margaret, just a half hour earlier, had burst into tears of joy when her two-month-old granddaughter, sleeping on her lap, had suddenly smiled and kung fu-gripped her na-na's finger. "So strong! So precious! And she smells like ambrosia! I can't stand it!"

But Tim's tears were different, his face contorted, his eyes evasive.

"The last thing I said to her was, 'Don't buy the *goddamned* light beer this time'," said Tim. "She hated it when I cursed. She just took the car keys and left without saying anything."

Consulting my earpiece at that moment would have been rude, so I dredged my brain and managed to pull a pertinent fact from the muck: Tim's wife had died in a car crash. "Irma," I said.

Tim's eyes snapped on to me. "Inga."

"Right! Inga. It was on New Year's Eve too, wasn't it? What, three years ago?"

"Five."

"Right. She was such a nice lady." I smiled at him and sat in a patio chair, which creaked under my weight, preparing to reminisce about Inga's bacon-spiked potato salad and seal-bark of a laugh.

Tim tilted his head to the side and gave me a quizzical look.

I froze. Had she been not so nice, her seal-bark cruel, her potato salad spiked not only with bits of salty pork fat but resentment and vindictiveness? Could my memory be that bad? But then Tim looked out on the lake and sighed, and a word came to me that had been absent from my vocabulary for years, which I had hardly heard spoken since I was a boy.

Sad.

Tim was sad. He was remembering his late wife on the fifth anniversary of her death, and it was making him feel sad.

I scooted my patio chair a few inches closer to Tim and lowered my voice. "Tim, are you feeling *sad*?"

He looked back at me. "You *do* remember."

I stood up. "I'll call an ambulance," I said, tapping my earpiece.

"No, goddammit!" Tim grabbed my arm and pulled me back into my seat. "I want... don't you see? I *want* to feel sad right now."

I studied his pleading face. Was this insanity? Sadness was a disease of the past, one of the worst, responsible for countless deaths and more senseless suffering than any other brain malfunction. It had been cured decades ago. I had gotten the nasal mist when I was eleven years old, and nowadays it was administered to one-year-olds along with their hepatitis A and cold vaccines.

Nobody *wanted* to feel sad.

Did they?

"I didn't know what to do with myself after she died," said Tim. "I mean, for a few days there were things to do, flowers to choose, an urn to buy. I didn't have to think; I just said 'sunflowers' whenever anyone asked me a question. 'Sunflowers for the memorial service? Are you sure?' they asked. 'Sunflowers,' I said. 'Sunflowers on the urn?' 'Yes, sunflowers.' She liked sunflowers, you know? It was something I was sure about." Tim took a long puff. "Maybe it was the only thing I was sure about. The lawyer... he had a stack of papers for me to sign with little yellow Post-it tabs poking out where my signatures were supposed to go. 'It's like a sunflower,' I said to him. He smiled and nodded. I thought he had done it on purpose. That's how feeble-minded I was at the time. I thought the nice lawyer had turned the paperwork into Inga's favorite flower."

I chuckled experimentally. Tim let out a wheeze that may or may not have been a laugh.

"Anyway, after the remembrances were done, and the papers were signed and filed, and the social media condolence pings had died down, I waited. I sat in an armchair, and I waited. I skipped my lifelong learning group, and I didn't go to the movies the way Inga and I used to do. I didn't go for hikes around the lake, even though I could have used the fresh air."

After a pause, I asked, "What were you waiting for?"

"That's just it, Glen. I didn't know *what* I was waiting for. It was like there was something I was going to do, but I couldn't remember what it was. And at some point I just forgot that I was waiting, and I resumed my life without ever having remembered what I was going to do. I took an ornithology class, and I bought some binoculars. I became a birder."

"Yeah, I heard that you—"

"What a dumb hobby that was. If I never see another rufous-bellied thrush it will be too soon."

"Oh."

"But I met another birder. Carmela. And, you know, sitting all day in a field with your binoculars and your bag of roasted cashews... Between almost spotting some fucking bird or other, it all came out. About Inga; about the light beer; about the yellow Post-its; about the waiting without knowing for what. And Carmela turned to me and said, 'Maybe you just need a good cry.' And then she said, 'Shhh,' and raised her binoculars, so I couldn't tell her how batshit crazy she was."

"Yeah."

"No, Glen. She wasn't crazy. As I sat there thinking, I realized she wasn't crazy. And then she asked me if I had heard of The Big S."

"The Big S?"

That was the first time I heard the drug's street name. It was usually called PIDS, an acronym of a complex, difficult to synthesize, and impossible to pronounce chemical. Some kids in Pittsburgh had been caught taking it.

On the ride home from the party, I leaned my forehead against the window and let my eyelids droop. The Big S. What was so big about it? My conversation with Tim had left me with an impression of something internalized but forgotten, like a dream whose details disintegrate in the morning light but whose pithy emotional core lingers through breakfast. It was enticing and frightening, and it smelled like... onions?

Clearly, I'd drunk too much champagne. I'd even asked Tim to put me in touch with his drug dealer. My wife would not approve.

I leaned towards her. "You know PIDS?"

"Pids?"

"You know, that drug…"

"Oh, right. The Big S." She shook her head. "It's so—"

"Hey, how do you know it's called The Big S?"

"What do you mean, how do I know? Everybody's talking about it."

"Everybody?"

"I just can't believe anyone would *want* to take it, you know? Imagine, *wanting* to feel *sad*."

I didn't respond.

"You know?" she prompted.

"Yeah." I said, while thinking to myself, *1212 18th Street. 1212 18th Street. 1212 18th Street.* The drug dealer's address, whispered by a birder in a bramble of blackberries to Uncle Tim, and passed along beside a moon-streaked lake to me. "Yeah."

1212 18th Street turned out to be a narrow, tinted-glass door tucked between a Noodles-2-Go and a mattress discount store. Scotch-taped inside the window above the door was an index card with the letter 'S' written in black marker, giving me confidence I had found the right place. I pressed the button five times in quick succession, as instructed, and peered into the nearly opaque glass. The door clicked. I pulled it open.

Leading up from the entryway was a burgundy-carpeted stairway, old but well-tended and lined by a brass railing, mottled with wear. On about the fifth step, high enough for her doleful eyes to be even with mine, sat a Cocker Spaniel. "Hello?" I said as I looked for evidence of a human presence. Finding none, I smiled at the dog's golden fur and long, ruffled ears. "Hey there, pup."

She turned to climb the stairs and I felt compelled to follow.

Red-paneled walls and yellowish lights gave the stairway a sinister, warm glow. I stopped on a landing after the first flight and the spaniel looked around. "Lead on, Virgil," I murmured. "Lead on." What was that from? Hamlet following the ghost? No. Dante, on the way to purgatory? Yes.

I entered a room lit with recessed sconces and furnished in antique cherry. The dog curled up at the foot of a velvet couch and huffed a sigh.

"Hello?" I said.

"Who is that, Daisy?" A silver-haired man entered the room from a dark hallway. "What have you dragged in off the street now?"

"Hello. I was given this address for... to get..."

"Yes, yes. Have a seat."

He didn't quite look at me, waving his hand dismissively. I hesitated, embarrassed, and suddenly wished I hadn't come. It was a bad idea after all. If my wife knew... But I was comforted by Daisy, lying croissant-like by the couch. I sat and leaned down to pet her.

The man reached to verify the existence of an armchair and lowered himself in. Blind, I guessed. He rested his hands on his knees. The cuffs of his shirt looked freshly ironed but slightly frayed. "So, first things first. Did you get the memo? No recording devices?"

"Yes," I said, distracted by the discoloration of his open shirt collar where it met his creased neck. "I mean no. No devices."

"No earpiece, no iris implant, no micropod?"

"I left it all at home."

"Good, good." His shoulders settled and his face softened. "So, you and Daisy are acquainted. My name is Bartholomew."

"I'm Glen."

"You came for The Big S, correct?"

"Yes."

"Good, good. How much do you want?"

"Uh…"

"You don't know, of course. You're a novice. Maybe you're not even sure you want it at all. Hmmm?"

"Well…"

"It's okay. Daisy, bring us a ten, please. Daisy, TEN." The dog didn't move. "She'll wait a moment just to prove to herself she's nobody's servant, and then she'll go get it. Watch." A note of warning entered his voice. "You're a good girl, aren't you, Daisy?" She got up and trudged from the room. "Yes, a very good girl."

"What a sweet dog."

"You try one, and if you like it, you buy the rest, okay? Simple, simple, simple. Free samples are key. Always. Have you ever sold drugs?"

"Me? No."

"You sound a little shocked by the question. Delicate soul. Ah, here's Daisy." The dog rattled back in with a bottle in her mouth, which she dropped in Bartholomew's outstretched hand. "Good girl." She slumped by the couch again, her body sounding like a small sack of potatoes being dropped on the wooden floor.

Bartholomew turned his face towards Daisy, and they sighed simultaneously. "She's a sad dog," he said. "And that sounds like I'm anthropomorphizing, but I'm not. She's had real sadness in her life."

"Oh?" I dug into the downy fur behind her ears to give her a good scritch. "Poor dog."

"What do you remember, Glen?" He shook the pill bottle. "About sadness."

"Not much, really. Just that..."

"Yes?"

"I was eleven when I went to the doctor for the mist, and my mother told me I wouldn't feel sad ever again. And that made me sad." Bartholomew raised his eyebrows. "I don't know why. Then I got the mist and I tried to hold on to the feeling, just to see if I could, but it was gone."

"Gone. Poof." He had a wry smile as he raised his hands magician-like in the air. "And what did feeling sad feel like? Do you remember that?"

"I really don't. That's what's been driving me crazy."

"Ah." He popped open the bottle and shook a pill onto his palm. "Well. So here we are. There's water on the coffee table."

I eyed the pill in the thin-fingered, slightly shaking hand. "How long does it last?"

"An hour, maybe two, the first time."

"The first time?"

"It builds up, so it goes on a little longer after that."

"Oh? Is it addictive?"

His hand dropped to rest on his knee, still holding the pill for me to take. "I don't think so."

That hung in the air for a moment.

"The Big S," said Bartholomew, clearing his throat, "has not been approved for sale by the Food and Drug Administration. I am not a board-certified pharmacologist. I offer no warranties, no assurances, no scientific studies showing short-term efficacy or long-term safety, no whitepapers, no testimonials beyond what the person who sent you here provided, without which you wouldn't be here, right?"

"Uh…"

"Word of mouth. That's another key to success in my line of work, along with free samples and making sure nothing gets recorded. But you didn't come here for drug-slinging advice. What you *came* for, what I *offer*," he shifted in his chair and leaned forward, "is that feeling your eleven-year-old self tried to hold onto but couldn't. That feeling that's too volatile, too dangerous, too *thrilling*," he closed his fist on the pill and pulled it away, "for society to let you feel it. You came here because you believe your feelings are your own to feel, that you can't be human without them, all of them, and this one," he opened his hand back up and pushed it in my general direction, "was stolen from you."

After a pause, I cleared my throat. "That was a good sales pitch."

"Thank you."

"I'll try it, of course." I leaned forward and took the pill. "It's what I came here for, I…" The tiny white hockey puck rolled on my palm.

"Yes?"

My feelings swirled: apprehension, curiosity, embarrassment, excitement. Bartholomew's creased brow tried to communicate openness and concern but couldn't hide an underlying impatience. "Never mind. Down the hatch!"

I popped the pill in my mouth and washed it down with water. I put down the glass and settled back on the couch.

"How long does it take?"

"A few minutes. Usually. While we wait, I could tell you about Daisy." Bartholomew crossed his arms and leaned his head to the side. "I find it helps set the mood."

"Okay."

"So, Daisy here was born to a Cocker Spaniel breeder in Greensboro, North Carolina. She was a friendly pup, or so I've heard, though she had a particular hatred for percolating coffee makers." He shrugged. "Still does; I switched to French press. Anyway, at eight months old, during her first heat, for reasons that were never explained to my satisfaction, the breeder thought it would be a good idea to breed Daisy with her father."

At the word 'father', I felt an unaccustomed tightening or twisting or burning sensation in my sternum and up around my rib cage. Like a lime being squeezed and the acidic juices leaking into my chest cavity.

"What?"

"Yes. Her father. Against all recommended breeding practices, moral codes, and plain old common sense, she was bred with her father while she was still, really, a puppy, and she got pregnant, and a couple months later she gave birth to something."

The feeling in my sternum spread out in thickening waves to my limbs.

"A poor, misshapen little something, that she clutched and cuddled and licked even though it showed no signs of life. When the breeder came to take it away and dispose of it, Daisy growled and whined, very out of character. She bit the breeder, hard, which would have gotten her put down but for the dram of compassion lingering in that breeder's shriveled heart."

The feeling grew heavy and warm — fleetingly, inadequately warm — like those lead jackets they used to make you wear when they x-rayed your teeth.

"That night, she howled out her pain, hour upon hour, while the breeder wore industrial grade foam earplugs she kept for just such occasions."

It was a big feeling. I groaned under its weight. The Big S.

"Daisy was not the same after that. She roamed the house in search of her lost baby. She was ruined for breeding, so she wound up at a shelter in Virginia, where I found her. Four years ago or so."

Looking at Daisy, watching the rise and fall of her breath, I slid off the couch and began to pet her from the crease in her forehead to the tip of her tail. She lifted her head at first in mild surprise, but then let it drop with a sigh.

"She had a sock. The shelter volunteer told me it had come with her from North Carolina. She would stow it in her bed and lick it in her quiet moments. I think it was her replacement baby. But we've lost it, and my socks aren't good enough for her, apparently. I've felt around, under the couches and chairs. It must be... but anyway, how are you coming along there, Glen?"

"Poor Daisy."

"Yes, yes. Poor Daisy. Ach, well, I may have embellished the story a bit over the years, but the general outline is accurate. If you do see a sock, a cotton athletic sock... But, you know, maybe I am anthropomorphizing a bit. Who knows what's in that little canine heart of hers?"

My hand paused on Daisy's back, and she raised her head to admonish me for slacking off. "What if the sock," I said, "was only a painful reminder?"

"Could be, could be."

Bartholomew folded his hands on his lap. From my vantage point on the floor his face looked distorted, like an ill-fitting mask. Tufts of salt-and-pepper hair poked from his nostrils. Under the coffee table I saw ratty slippers, toes poking through a broken seam.

I refocused my attention on Daisy and probed the width and breadth and height of my drug-induced sadness. I had thought that I would burst into tears, but that didn't happen. The feeling was comfortable, familiar, satisfying even, like picking a dried scab on my knee as a kid.

I was eleven again, holding the feeling close, watching my mother's face as she watched mine. Watching her watch the creases in my brow smooth out. Watching her watch me watch the worry in her eyes fade away.

Remembering her, pre-mist, lying beside me on my bed, shushing me softly, and at the same time encouraging my tears. A boy had pushed me while I was at the urinal, and I sprayed pee on the floor. The other boys laughed like cartoon donkeys. They hated me. "No," she said. "You're my sweet little boy. Let it out. It's okay." Let it out, get it out, spill it out...

Remembering another night when daddy said mommy was feeling sad. I tried to comfort her the way she had comforted me. "You're my beautiful mommy," I said. "It's okay. Let it out, mommy. Get it out." Her eyes dry and blank, not letting it out. Her body a lead weight, so heavy I thought I would roll into the well she made there on the bed. Daddy in a chair with his hands on his face, dragging them down. "I love you," he said to mommy, like an accusation, almost.

Let it out, get it out, spit it out, work it out...

I love you, but...

The edge of a bottomless pit...

Visiting mommy in the hospital, the machine with the colored graphs and lights and numbers, the needle in her arm, the smell of medicine and doctors, dim gray lights in the ceiling, watching her watch me watch her watch me...

Daddy, taking her hand. "I should have locked up the pills," he said.

Locked up the pills…

I love you, but…

Sliding, grasping, flailing, falling… my very own pit… my eyes dry and blank.

Later, after the mist, walking into the kitchen, and daddy saying to mommy, "Well, it saved your life." He diced onions while mommy stirred something in a pot on the stove.

"Maybe," she said.

Daddy scraped the onions into the pot. He sniffled and rubbed his eyes. It was the onions. It was just the onions that made that happen now. He placed the cutting board on the edge of the sink and laid the knife across it, its blade flashing.

I realized that this memory had been an unanswered question lodged in a crevice in the back of my mind all these years. What had saved her life? The mist?

"Bartholomew, what about sadness that is *too* strong or lasts *too* long?"

He had been sitting stoically, hands folded on his lap, hairy-knuckled thumbs twiddling. How much time had passed? He opened his mouth but paused a moment before answering. "It's a risk, but I haven't heard any complaints."

I scooped my hand under Daisy's body as I stroked her from head to tail, head to tail, head to tail. Her eyelids fluttered. Little by little, the sadness lifted, until I found myself cooing and chirping, "What a nice dog you are, Daisy."

"So," said Bartholomew, "what do you think?"

I blinked at him. The feeling was gone, but the dark cloud of memory lingered. I got up and sat back down on the couch and eyed the pill bottle on the coffee table between us.

"Quite an experience, right?"

"Yes. Wow. Quite an experience."

"So, I accept Q-bucks or Singaporean Aphids." He leaned down and retrieved a card reader from a drawer in the side of the coffee table.

"Well, I..."

"You can start with the ten, or I do have the thirty-thirty deal — 30 percent off a bottle of thirty. That's three times the experience for only twice the 'phids." He tapped the card reader on the edge of the table.

"I don't..."

"You don't what?"

The leaden weight; the eyes watching, hoping, fearing; the slippery-edged pit. "I don't think I want them."

"You don't *think*?"

"I mean, it's quite an experience, as you say... but for me, it's not a good idea."

"Not a —" The card reader clattered on the table as Bartholomew leaned back and crossed his arms. "Daisy, bite him. Bite Glen on the ankle for wasting your master's time. Go on. Daisy, BITE."

Daisy rose and yawned nervously. She looked from Bartholomew to me and back again.

"She won't bite you, will she? She thinks she's not my servant, doesn't she? But who feeds you? Huh?"

Daisy sniffed my pant leg and nudged my hand with her nose.

"I should have stuck with smack and weed." Slapping his knees and rising, Bartholomew sang under his breath. "*Weed and smack and a little bit o' crack. The good ol' days.*" He left the room, knocking his knee on a chair and cursing softly, bitterly. "Fuck."

I rose to apologize, to say goodbye, to say something — maybe to say I'd buy the pills after all. Nothing came out of my mouth. Instead, I knelt down to pet Daisy some more.

"I'd better go, Daisy."

I wanted to get out before Bartholomew came back. With Daisy at my heel, I headed for the stairs. By the door, a rolled-up sock behind a vase on an eye-level shelf caught my eye.

"Oh. A sock. Could this be...?"

I lifted it off the shelf, and Daisy tensed. She sat and pinned the sock with her gaze.

I had theorized earlier that the sock had been an unwelcome reminder. Maybe it would be better for Daisy if I put it back on the shelf? But with her intent, pleading eyes drilling a hole in my hand, that was out of the question. Would it dredge up sorrowful memories of unfulfilled motherhood, or would it soothe the ache of a barren womb? If she could speak, could she explain it? Would I understand? Or did she only know she wanted it?

And what about me, retreating, tail tucked, to a present of forgetful bliss?

I held the sock in front of her snout, and she enveloped it in her mouth. I let go, and she rushed behind the velvet couch and out of sight.

"You're a brave soul," I said, turning to descend the stairs.

*See David Hammond's story "The Big S" online at Metaphorosis.*
*If you liked it, leave a comment. Authors love that!*
*Remember to subscribe to our e-mail updates so you'll know when new stories are posted.*

## About the story

This story started with me thinking about the current state of drug therapies for depression. Basically, I wished antidepressants worked better.

That wish segued naturally into a series of escalating thought experiments: What if there were a cure for depression? What if that cure didn't just affect clinical depression, but ordinary sadness, and it were given to everyone? What if, after sadness was eradicated, someone developed a drug for people to feel sad again? Would people take it?

Of course they would.

But I thought there was enough complexity in how it would play out to explore in a story, and I quickly hit on the idea of exploring the relationship between emotion and memory. Cutting off emotions can empty out memories either by making them inaccessible or robbing them of meaning, and losing memories can make emotions incomprehensible. And sometimes confronting the emotional content of memories is a choice. When do we choose to feel, choose to remember, and when do we choose to lock it away in an act of self-preservation? Is denying an emotion ever the right thing to do?

At some point in working on the story, I got a vision of a dog as a drug dealer's side-kick, and a great deal of my motivation from then on was to write about this dog, to make the dog an important character in the story while keeping her a real dog. So Daisy was born. I made her a Cocker Spaniel because my vision included big ruffly ears.

## A question for the author

**Q:** What would your characters say about you?

**A:** I forwarded this question to the characters from "The Big S," and here are their responses:

Glen: David Hammond... David Hammond... Nope, doesn't ring a bell.

Tim: He hardly says a word most of the time, but if you liquor him up and land on the right subject, he'll talk your ear off.

Bartholomew: I contracted him to do my website, www.getthebigs.com. I thought he did a decent job until I heard from some of my clients. Either he was taking advantage of me being blind, or his design skills are shit.

Daisy: *brings ball, puts ball at feet, looks up with big brown eyes and pants expectantly, nudges ball with nose in case you didn't notice it*

## About the author

David Hammond lives and dreams in Virginia with his wife, two daughters, one dog, three rats, and a multitude of insects. During the day, he makes websites.

oldshoepress.com, @hammond13

# The Otherside of Memory

Kelly Sandoval

*Lord Rivenwend of the North Star and Lady Siverstay of the Sun's Dawning*
    *Request the honor of your presence at the marriage of their son*
    *Lord Creythwin the Dawn Star*
    *To*
    *Teresa the Fair of the Cleaved Land*
    *Windsday, the 39th of Harvest*
    *Dusk*
    *To attend, jump through a puddle of still water during the next full moon*
    *P.S. Please come, Katie. I don't think I can face this without you. Love, T.*

*Please come.* Teresa made it sound so simple. As if more than fifteen years, and that last bitter fight, could be swept away like soap bubbles on the wind. As if one world were just as good as the next.

Kate set the invitation down on top of the pile of more conventional mail she'd been sorting. Bills, pre-approved credit cards, coupon mailers. All the simple, mundane business of the world she'd chosen. Teresa probably had her mail delivered by helpful woodland creatures. Which was fine for her, but Kate preferred her mail without tooth marks and urine stains.

*Please come.* Just like that. Not even an apology. No recognition of what'd come after, what it'd been like to be the one who came back. What did Teresa think happened, when you entered the woods with your best friend, and returned, days later, alone and dressed in velvet rags?

Kate picked up the invitation again, noting the elegant pearlescence of the paper, the way it seemed to glow. Then she tore it into tiny, gleaming squares, wrapped it in coupons, and threw it in the trash.

If Teresa couldn't face marrying whiny, clingy Crey alone, maybe she should call off the wedding.

"Sorry, Teresa," she said aloud, remembering how they used to spy on their parents through magic mirrors. "I'm busy."

Leaving the bills for later, she turned her attention to the window. Charlotte was on the porch, driving a toy truck through a crowd of plastic houses. Such a practical girl, these days. The princess tantrums had been hard, but they'd gotten through it. Charlotte understood better now, how foolish such things were. No lies about Santa, no creepy voyeuristic elves. Instead of slipping coins under Charlotte's pillow, Kate had sat her daughter down, and they'd worked out a fair market value for baby teeth.

It had been harder, before Tom left. He'd insisted on whimsy. Such fights they'd had. He'd refused to understand, and she hadn't been able to explain.

There were doors out there. Doors waiting for Charlotte, just like they'd waited for Kate. If they didn't teach her to scorn the dreams those doors promised, they could lose her to one. At best she'd come back a different child, with a lifetime behind her eyes. At worst... well, not all children came back.

But Kate hadn't been able to explain all that. Hadn't been able to tell Tom that in her nightmares, Charlotte wandered down an endless hallway, each door opening as she passed.

In the end, divorce had felt like the only option. Sometimes, children required sacrifice.

Charlotte was late coming down for breakfast the next morning. Kate found her sitting in her room, piecing the invitation back together. She'd almost finished, and the note gleamed in front of her, the horse along the border running as far as it could along the broken line of its track.

"Look!" Charlotte stared up at her, all smiles. "Isn't it pretty?"

"Where'd you find that?" The words came out sharper than Kate intended, and Charlotte's smile fell.

"Here," she said. "I just sorta found it."

"Your cereal's getting soggy." Kate nodded toward the door. "Get downstairs. I'll clean this up."

"But—"

"Now, Charlotte."

"Fine." Charlotte's tone, and the way she stomped to the door, merited further discussion, but Kate let it pass.

Kneeling to pick up the scraps, she saw that they'd already begun to knit themselves back together. Only a few pieces, along the top edge, were still missing. She scanned the invitation out of habit, eyes coming to rest on the P.S.

*P.S. Katie, please. You promised. I'm scared. T*

Teresa, the bold one. Teresa, who ran through doors to other worlds, dragging Kate behind her. Teresa who swore she would never return, no matter what. Who left Kate to stumble back alone, through the darkness, with no words to explain what had happened to them.

What did Kate care if she was scared? And still, her shoulders tensed when she read the words, bracing as if to protect someone from a blow.

"Mommy!" Charlotte called, from downstairs.

Kate fitted the last few pieces of the invitation into their place, and watched it stitch itself whole. Then she folded it neatly and slid it into the back pocket of her jeans.

How could she even think of going? It wasn't like she could leave Charlotte alone while she went chasing old pain through moonlit pools.

And to take her? Make truth of every nightmare? Ridiculous.

But the idea lingered. Despite her best efforts, the lure of the otherside, of an open door, still felt inevitable. And the more Charlotte grew, the less she could protect her. But if she could go with her, maybe she could make it safe. Guide her attention to the pathetic falseness of it all.

Charlotte was a practical girl, when she was home. Less so, around her father. And who knew what she might be like, if she wandered alone through an open door. But if Kate were with her? Well.

It was three days until the full moon. She had time to decide.

"But what about Rosy?" Charlotte asked, tugging at Kate's hand as they walked toward the local park.

It was well past sunset, but the suburban streetlights were mostly blocking the stars, leaving the moon, full and round, to light the sky.

"Rosy will be fine," Kate answered, not for the first time. She'd already arranged for the neighbors to check in on the little pug. She'd promised to be back in a few days, a week at most. Surely, it wouldn't take longer than that. It hadn't been, last time. Taking Charlotte to an old friend's wedding, she'd told them. True enough. It was a wedding, at least.

"And we're going to see horses?"

"Oh, yes. Horses until you want to scream." They'd reached the edge of the park; Kate could see the fountain's pool shining in the moonlight. "Things are very different where my friend lives. You understand?"

"Try foods. Don't call things weird. No faces." Charlotte ticked the usual rules off on her fingers, and Kate freed her hand to smooth her daughter's dark curls.

"I want you to see this, because—"

Because?

Because there would always be the risk of doors, in Charlotte's life. Always be the chance that she'd hear some distant music and find herself dancing, dreamlike, across a threshold. Despite all Kate's best attempts, Charlotte still doodled fairies in the corners of her schoolwork. There was still a danger.

But this way, she could turn the otherside into just another boring errand, robbed of all its forbidden, escapist charm. Charlotte could be level-headed and practical, with the right sort of guidance. With Kate beside her, she would see all the bright whimsy for the shallow artifice it was.

"Mommy?" Charlotte tugged at her sleeve. "Because why?"

"I don't know, hon. Just because."

The fountain was only a handbreadth away now. The spray of it filled the air, misting gently down on them. Kate adjusted her bag and stared down into the basin, where the ripples settled under her attention, the reflected moon coming clear. Full and round and opening before them like the door. She could hear laughter and the sweet, sharp music of the otherside. Charlotte tried to pull away from her, yearning toward the sound, while Kate stood rooted in place.

This was it.

Gripping Charlotte more tightly, Kate squared her shoulders and stepped forward, into the bright portal of the moon. She didn't even feel the water, just a rushing, silver coolness and the warmth of Charlotte's hand, as the world went bright.

"Katie!" Teresa's voice was just as Kate remembered, all low, soft sweetness. "Oh, Katie, thank god!"

The world came back into focus. Well, not *the* world so much as *a* world. The otherside, all dressed for autumn, with endless rolling hills of copper fire. The palace like a Disney dream in the field beyond. And there was Teresa, looking no older than she'd been when Kate left, just barely twenty. The age Kate had left behind when she returned home and found herself shedding years like dreams.

She hadn't known, in going back, that she'd have to live the years from 12 to 20 again. It had been harder, the second time. One more thing this place had done to her.

Teresa stood in her filmy, silken gown, shifting nervously from foot to foot, watching Kate with a helpless sort of hope.

Kate had run through what happened next dozens of times. She'd rehearsed her words, won imaginary arguments, and considered how to say 'I forgive you' in a sufficiently magnanimous and superior fashion.

Her mouth was dry, and she could remember none of it.

"Mom?" Charlotte was coming out of the trance of otherside's music, her eyes wide as she took in the lush, impossible beauty of the landscape. A herd of horses, with snow-white hides and manes like flame, were running past along the hills, and Charlotte's eyes followed them with naked longing. "Mommy where are they going? Will we get to pet them?"

"Maybe later," Kate managed to say. "Say hello to my friend. This is Miss Teresa."

"But *you* didn't say hi."

"Hi, Teresa," she said, forcing a smile. "It's been a long time."

"I'm Charlotte," said Charlotte.

"A kid?" Teresa asked. "We never— you always said—"

"You're marrying Crey." Kate stood a little straighter, meeting Teresa's gaze as fiercely as she could. "So I don't think you can talk."

Kate braced herself for one of Teresa's clever, sharp-edged retorts.

Instead, Teresa flinched, and lowered her eyes. "Yeah. Things change. Even here."

That old urge, the product of a shared childhood and a secret lifetime, almost pulled Kate forward, to comfort and question and try to fix. But she'd already tried to save Teresa, had opened the way back and asked her to follow. It hadn't worked.

"Why am I here?" she asked, tightening her grip on Charlotte's hand.

Teresa smiled, bright and untroubled, and the moment's tension faded. "You're my maid of honor. We can hardly have the wedding without you."

The dress Teresa wanted Kate to wear was exactly the sort of faux-princess monstrosity that she and Teresa would have imagined as children. Layers of velvet and satin, wide, trailing sleeves, and all of it in the deepest of gem tones, dark blues and purples that shimmered even by candlelight.

It took three people just to get her in it. They stood around her, cooing and complimenting, all of them beautiful and soft-voiced and alike in that strange, unsettling way that defined the otherside.

"Mommy, you're a princess," said Charlotte, as measurements were made and pins were pinned. "Will I get to be a princess too?"

"I'm not a princess," Kate corrected immediately. "Just your mom, in a fancy dress. And yes, you get to wear one too. It'll probably be scratchy and hot, just like this one."

"That's okay." Charlotte sounded unintimidated by the threat of discomfort, which just went to show that the otherside was working its magic. Most days, it was hard to get her to so much as agree to a sweater.

"If you could raise your arm," said the blonde-haired, angelic-faced woman on Charlotte's right. "We're almost done."

Kate lifted her arm, twisting to face her. Their eyes met. The woman's, an unusual blue-green, caught and held hers. Teresa's sister had those same eyes. Growing up, they'd always been jealous of her, had tried to wish their eyes to a new shade, staring endlessly at pictures of Teresa's sister and hoping, hoping, hoping.

The woman started pinning again, and Kate looked away.

"Where's Teresa?"

"She's with her fiancé, ma'am," one of the other women answered immediately. "Would you like me to send for her?"

"That's not necessary."

In the old days, it wouldn't have been. If she'd wanted Teresa, she could have looked in any mirror, and found her. In the old days, she'd have known where Teresa was the same way she knew the beating of her own heart. Now, closing her eyes, she felt nothing. The otherside was Teresa's, no longer a shared magic. It was surely the better for it.

Kate's memories of her last year in the otherside were still uncomfortably vivid. Claustrophobic and restless, exhausted by the endless sameness, and longing for home, she'd soured on everything she'd once admired. Ever obliging, the world had twisted, growing crueler and closer to reflect her sense of it.

"Can I play with your phone?" Charlotte asked. She'd clearly tired of the scraps of ribbon that the women had given her to entertain herself.

"It's in my purse, hon. But most of the games won't work. They don't have Wi-Fi here." There was no harm in letting Charlotte use it until it ran down. It wasn't like they'd be making any calls. "And we can't charge it either."

"Why not?" Charlotte asked.

"No electricity." It seemed a good time to push the point. "No TV, no video games. No phones."

"Internet?"

"Nope."

"But how do they—" Charlotte paused, overwhelmed by the enormity of the lack. "How do they do anything?"

"They don't. Pretty boring, huh?"

Charlotte looked from the phone to the ridiculous dress the women were constructing around Kate. "Yeah," she said hesitantly. "Pretty boring."

"Would you like me to take her down to the menagerie, ma'am?" The woman who'd given Charlotte the ribbons asked. She looked a little older than the others, about Kate's age. A 12-year-old's idea of all grown up.

"No thanks." But despite herself, Kate flashed the woman a grateful smile. It was always nice to have someone willing to pitch in. "I'll take her down later. Maybe with Teresa."

"I'm sure she'd enjoy that." The woman stepped close to her, pitching her voice in that low, quiet way that spoke of secrets, or worry. "Ma'am?"

Kate let her arm drop as the one with the familiar eyes finished pinning. "Hmm?"

"This is your second visit. You—" The woman paused, looking away. "You still remember, don't you? What it was like, the last time?"

"More than I'd like to."

"You should go back to the old places. The ones you remember best. It would be nice, don't you think? To visit the shadow gardens again. To show your daughter the silver lakes and the forest of songs."

The words felt like an old wound, reopened. Kate had curated her memories of the otherside, clinging to the worst of it, to those last painful months. The places the woman spoke of, well, it wasn't that she'd forgotten. But she tried not to think of them. She didn't want to see the shadow gardens again, didn't want to swim in the sweet, glittering waters of the silver lakes. She wanted to wear an itchy, tacky dress, glare at Crey, and go home. She wanted to collect a new list of reasons to hate this place, and she wanted

Charlotte to languish in boredom, longing for television and her friends.

"I'm not sure there'll be time," she said.

The woman turned away from the window. "Of course," she said, with a forced, helpless brightness. "I didn't mean to impose on your time, ma'am. I only thought the little girl might like to see where her mother grew up."

"Mommy grew up in Ohio," Charlotte said. "We go there for Christmas. It's boring. Grandma doesn't let us bring Rosy."

"Grandma's allergic," Kate put in firmly. "Is your game working?"

"Yeah. When do we pet the horses?"

"After we're done here, hon."

"Could you stand a little straighter?" The older woman knelt, ready with pins of her own. Her tone was neutral, and she didn't look up as she spoke.

Kate straightened, pushing down a flash of unexpected guilt. Could you really be said to have hurt something from the otherside? Perhaps, in the same way Charlotte could worry over the feelings of her stuffed animals, rotating them out nightly so that none felt left out.

"What's to see at the silver lakes?" she asked.

The woman was silent for long enough that Kate assumed she wasn't going to answer. One of the others began to sing, and while the words were strange, the tune was familiar.

"I couldn't say, ma'am," the woman said at last. "No one much goes down there, anymore."

No one? In Kate's memory, the shores were bright with people. They'd gone out on little boats, had picnics in the center of the lake. Dived deep, and come out gleaming.

Something felt wrong. The woman's voice. Or the idea of the shining lakes gone silent. The palace, so much less grand than she remembered. Hollowed out.

"Maybe I will pay them a visit," she said.

"But horses," Charlotte objected.

"The horses can wait, Charlotte. Besides, I'm a little allergic to horses. You don't want me all itchy and sneezy, do you?" Of course, an otherside horse was about as likely to trigger a reaction as a My Little Pony, but Charlotte didn't need to know that.

"But you promised!" The sharp hint of a whine entered Charlotte's words. It was comforting, almost. If she could throw a fit here, clearly the otherside's glamour hadn't penetrated too deeply.

"And we will see them. After we go to the lakes."

"But—"

"Charlotte, if you keep this up, we can go home right now." Well, eventually. The moon wasn't up. Kate only knew the route by moonlight.

"Ma'am, I could take her down to the stables, if you like." The woman who'd spoken of the lakes offered. "While you enjoy the water."

"That's very kind, umm—"

"Verita, ma'am."

"Verita, I appreciate the offer, but I have no intention of letting my daughter out of my sight."

"The horses are quite tame."

Kate looked down at Charlotte, that hopeful, hungry expression on her face. "That's not the danger I'm concerned about. I'll take her to the stables myself."

"We'll really go?" Charlotte asked. "You don't have to pet them if you're allergic."

"We'll go. But first, we have to meet Teresa for lunch. After that, we'll go down to the lakes, and then the horses."

"Fine." Charlotte sat back down with a huff, placated if not exactly happy. "This isn't as fun as you said it'd be."

Kate found herself smiling. "Charlotte, hon, I didn't say it'd be fun at all."

Kate had expected Teresa to hold their lunch in the formal dining room. Long, dark wood tables, soft-voiced servants, perhaps someone playing a half-remembered pop song on a lute. She'd imagined their voices echoing across a ridiculously long table, any real conversation rendered impossible.

Instead, the man who came to fetch them led the way to the kitchen gardens, a close, cozy area, the air sweet with herbs. Teresa was sitting on a blanket under a red-leafed maple tree, Crey at her side.

Like Teresa, he looked much the same as he had when she left. Recklessly handsome, with dark eyes and the feathered hair of an 80s dreamboat. The eyes were softer, though. The lopsided smile, dopey but warm.

"There you are!" He rushed forward, pulling her into a hug before she could object, ever the over-excited sidekick, too eager for affection. "I knew you would come. Didn't I say? I did. You'll stay, won't you? We've missed you so!"

"Just until the wedding," Kate and Teresa said, both at once, in the same, long-suffering tones. Teresa smiled though, patting the spot next to her. When he sat down, he kissed her cheek.

"How was the fitting?" Teresa asked, as she unpacked a basket full of cakes and tarts and pies and, well, everything Kate would ordinarily tell Charlotte was 'sometimes food'.

"Is that really lunch?" Charlotte tugged Kate forward, eyes wide and hopeful.

"I'm afraid so," Kate replied, settling on the blanket. "Don't eat yourself sick."

They made small talk for a while. Dresses. Flowers. Crey's new passion for cooking. (It was always something. Often, whatever could best get him into trouble. Mermaids, dragon's eggs, phoenix watching. Cooking seemed a safe, even charmingly domestic, hobby. In some ways, perhaps, Teresa was growing up.) Charlotte soon grew bored and lay stretched out on the grass, drowsily making daisy chains and ignoring them.

"And of course, there will be dancing!" Crey was saying, with inexhaustible enthusiasm. "You remember the balls we used to have, don't you Katie? Like the one where the wyverns attacked, and I—"

"I remember." Kate admitted, carefully keeping her tone neutral. They had been fun, of course. Ridiculous dresses, jeweled masks, and always the right dash of adventure, anytime the experience grew dull. "We don't have many dances, back home."

"You must miss it," he said, and she wasn't sure whether his tone was wistful or wheedling.

She had, at first. Despite her desperate need to escape and the inevitable pain of return. She'd spent those early months of therapy longing for her lost friend, her lost world. With time, the want grew bitter.

"Eventually, you have to let things go," she said.

"That's giving up," Teresa replied, meeting her gaze.

The same argument they'd fought again and again, with increasing urgency, in the days before Kate finally left. She'd begged Teresa to come with her. Threatened. Made impossible promises. And Teresa had done the same, trying to keep her.

At least now, they could simply sketch the shape of the old battles, without fighting them again.

"I missed you," Kate said, meaning, it's not *you* I gave up on.

"I'm sure you made new friends," Teresa replied. Meaning what? That she, alone on the otherside, could not do the same?

"Eventually," Kate admitted. "I didn't talk to many people at first. My parents thought I'd been kidnapped. They kept me home. Brought in a therapist."

"I saw." Teresa's voice was soft. "I'm sorry."

And wasn't that what she'd been waiting to hear? But Kate couldn't find the words to reply, not with recrimination or acceptance. She watched Teresa stare at her hands, and all she wanted to do was hold them in her own, take the hurt from her eyes. Make it better.

But she didn't even belong to the same world. Not anymore.

"I promised we'd go for a walk after lunch," she said, tugging at Charlotte's shoe to get her attention. "I'll see you both at dinner."

It was easier to leave than risk more fighting. It always had been.

The walk to the silver lakes was so uneventful that Kate felt nearly as bored as Charlotte, who stomped along at her side. The woods were quiet, and the autumn leaves drifted around them as they walked, a dry rain of red and gold. She'd never seen the otherside in autumn before. In her memory, there were endless summer days and winter snows, but no new budding flowers or falling leaves. She couldn't help but marvel at the beauty of it all, and wonder, a little, at what it might mean. Why autumn now, for Teresa's wedding? Why not blooming roses and baby animals?

"Where are the birds?" Charlotte asked. "And the squirrels?"

"I don't know, hon. They used to be everywhere."

The walk was shorter than Kate remembered. Within half an hour, they'd almost reached the lakes. The trees were thinning, though the woods stayed silent, no distant sounds of people or waterfowl. The ground grew rocky underfoot, as they pushed through the last of the trees. That, at least, was familiar. The lakes had always appeared like a surprise, between one bend and the next.

The lakes were gone.

Not merely dry, but missing, replaced by a vast stretch of parched, flat land. The shores had gleamed once, stones like gems and silver sand. Nothing now. Just an expanse of gray rocks.

"Mommy, are we almost there?" Charlotte asked.

And Kate, staring out across where the water wasn't, couldn't find an answer. What had happened? How could the lakes just stop being?

She let go of Charlotte's hand and sat down on the rocks. She wanted to close her eyes, to shut it all out. Forgetting the lakes was one thing. Losing them, like this, was something else. They had been so happy here, once.

"Mommy?" Charlotte's hand was warm on her shoulder. "Mommy, what's wrong? Are we lost? Do we need to call a police officer? I didn't use all the phone."

"We're not lost." Kate's voice shook a little. She took a slow breath before trying again. "I'm just tired. I'm going to sit for a bit. Stay where I can see you. Then we can go see the horses."

Charlotte sat nearby, humming to herself and stacking stones while Kate stared, helpless, out at the absence of the lakes.

"I didn't come here anymore, after you left." Teresa's voice startled her out of her mourning. She jumped to her feet, turning to see Verita leading a black horse down the path. Teresa sat on the horse's back, in a fine blue riding dress.

Kate stood silent, hunting for words. No use asking how Teresa had found her. Even without Verita's help, she'd always know where Kate, and everyone, was.

"Mommy, a horse!" Charlotte said, jumping to her feet. She ran straight at the animal, who lowered its head and nuzzled her in immediate affection.

Horses on the otherside were like that. Unless you didn't want them to be.

"This is Winterwind," said Teresa, sliding off the horse's back. "She could be your horse, if you like, Charlotte."

"Oh, Mommy, could we? Could I please?"

"And are you going to shovel the poop and ride it every day and go out at five in the morning to feed it before school?"

"I could." Charlotte sat a little straighter. "Mommy, you never let anything be fun."

"That's not true."

Teresa laughed, not kindly. "Your mom's always been very serious."

Not always. She'd helped make this place, once.

"We'll talk about the horse later," Kate said at last. Now wasn't the time for that argument.

"I can ride her though, right?"

"I suppose. With help."

"Verita, why don't you take Charlotte around the clearing?" Teresa asked. "Winterwind will appreciate the exercise."

"Stay where I can see you," Kate said. "Teresa and I will talk."

Verita helped Charlotte onto the horse, then climbed on behind her. Kate watched as the horse made its gentle, ambling way, its tail streaming out behind it with more drama than its pace really required. Charlotte's laughter filled the air, sweet as the birds that weren't singing.

"We used to ride here," Teresa said, coming to stand closer to Kate.

"We used to do a lot of things." Kate kept her gaze locked on the empty expanse where the lake wasn't. "What happened here, Teresa?"

"Nothing." Teresa threw a stone, and it fell dead in the dust beside one of the shrubs, shaking free a few dry leaves. "Nothing happened here, after you left. And eventually there wasn't a here anymore."

"But we loved the lakes." Kate hated the sorrow in her words, but the grief wouldn't be buried. There'd been a time when she really believed that she and Teresa would live forever in the otherside, sister queens ruling over a land that bent to suit their every whim.

"It's not just here," Teresa said, playing nervously with the hem of her shirt. "The shadow gardens are gone. The forest of songs is still there, but the trees only sing the same song, over and over again. I don't think they'll last much longer. Sometimes, the servants all have the same face. And they all look like me. I can't keep it all in my head, Katie. I can't care about all of it, all the time."

She might have closed the space between them, then. Might have pulled Teresa close, let her cry, even cried with her. Friends did that sort of thing.

"You had to know this was coming," she said. "This isn't a place you stay, Teresa. You can't have a life here. Not a real life."

"I could. If you stayed. You and Charlotte both."

Charlotte and Verita were finishing their first circuit of the missing lake. The horse came trotting toward them, and for a moment, Kate couldn't tear her eyes away. Had she ever seen her daughter so ecstatic?

"Mommy, look! Mommy, I'm riding!"

"I see you, hon," Kate called back. "You're doing great."

"She'd be happy, here," Teresa said, after the horse had passed.

"You know we're not staying." At last, Kate turned to look at Teresa.

Teresa's eyes were bright with the threat of tears, but she stood, back straight, trying to smile. "I know. But I had to ask."

"You could come back with us." Though what that meant, Kate wasn't sure. Would Teresa be 12 again, as Kate had been? Would she return to the past? How could she, when Kate had already lived those years alone?

"And what would happen to this place, if I left?"

"It's not real."

"Of course it—" Teresa's words were just on the edge of shouting, but she cut herself off, biting her lip and staring at her feet. "Maybe we made them. Maybe we made all of it. But that doesn't mean they're not real. They have feelings. Good days and bad days. They die. They mourn. They are real, Katie. And they're our—they're my responsibility. If I leave, it all falls into ruin. I can't do that to them."

"You said they're already fading."

"That's why I have to save the ones I can." She glanced back up, offering a watery smile. "I guess I thought, if you saw what it'd come to here, you might want to help."

Kate held out her arm, and Teresa stepped close. She was shaking, and for a second, Kate loved her as much as she ever had. Her best friend. The two of them lost, hurt, and ready to take on the world together. To make a world together, if that's what it took to feel safe. Kate hiding from her mother's anger and her father's absence. Teresa washing away under an endless list of expectations, a bar that moved higher every time her fingers brushed it. And then a door, and a song, and a lifetime.

She'd left Teresa. She'd had to leave her. When the world grew poisoned with her own restless bitterness, when the fruit rotted and the servants grew snide. When, suddenly, there was horse shit in the stables, and Crey, always amusingly obnoxious, grew menacing. What choice was there, then?

"I'm sorry, Teri."

"What am I supposed to do?" Teresa asked. Despite her shaking, her voice was steady.

Come back, Kate wanted to say. Come with me. I'll protect you. You'll be Charlotte's big sister. We'll be best friends. Whatever you owe this place, you don't owe it this.

She stroked her friend's arm, leaning so her cheek rested against her hair.

"Keep fighting. And I'll come again. If it helps. If you want to see me."

"I can't open the door often," Teresa replied. "I don't know what'll be left, next time. It might just be me."

"Then we'll go back together."

Charlotte and Verita came round again, and Teresa stepped away, brushing at her dress. "Your daughter's lovely, you know. She reminds me of you. Her father?"

"No one you know. We're divorced."

"Oh. I— sorry."

"Don't be," Kate said. "Sometimes, people just aren't meant to stay together, you know?"

Teresa laughed. "Oh, yeah. I get that."

"You and Crey?" Kate asked.

Teresa's smile didn't fade, though she shook her head in helpless, amused denial. "He's Crey, you know? Our perpetual fanboy. Everything that ever irritated us, just so we'd have someone to be irritated with."

"From experience, I can't say that's the best basis for a marriage."

"He's the realest one here, Katie. The one we paid the most attention to. Half our adventures, he was with us. The other half, we were trying to save him. I guess I'm still trying to save him."

The horse had reached them again, and this time, Verita slowed it to a stop. Kate stepped forward, and Charlotte slipped off into her arms.

"Don't you want to ride, Mommy?"

"Sorry, hon." Kate ran her fingers through her daughter's wind-tangled hair, trying to pat it back into order. "We've gotta help Aunt Teresa get ready for her wedding, ok?"

"More itchy dresses?"

"I'm sure they won't be that itchy. And there's a cake, and flowers, and I bet Aunt Teresa will even ride her horse Moonfall down the aisle."

"And you'll ride Everstar?" Teresa asked, rubbing at her eyes.

"Of course."

The wedding was everything it had to be. A fairytale impossibility, the bridal party on horses, doves singing the wedding march, and Teresa a confection of white, riding down an aisle that Charlotte had enthusiastically coated in scarlet petals. Even Crey did his part, strikingly handsome in his black suit and short cape.

Teresa said her vows, making a promise to protect Crey, to stand by his side, to serve the otherside for as long as she lived.

As long as it lived, Kate thought, and she let herself cry. Why not? Everyone wept at weddings.

In the celebration that followed, as Charlotte ran from table to table with giddy abandon, Kate sat alone, watching them all. The parents of the groom still held the sparks of stars, their skin gleaming under their wedding silks. Verita and the other servants exchanged toasts and stole bites of food from each other's plates. Crey kept looking over at Teresa, awestruck. As if, even with the wedding over, he couldn't quite believe that she'd picked him.

And they were all real. And they were none of them more than what Teresa needed them to be. No one stepped on her dress, or started messy, drunken fights. Only Charlotte, running with a plate full of cake, caused any sort of chaos.

Kate felt the old itch, the longing to get away from the otherside, with its patterns and its predictability. To go back to a world that didn't care about her, if only to be surprised. She drank her wine, and she watched Teresa, and she waited for the moon.

The party had quieted, and Charlotte lay drowsing in Kate's arms, when the moon finally reached its peak, and the silver path lay clear before her. Kate stood, cradling Charlotte close, and picked up the bag she'd tucked discreetly under the table. Teresa pulled away from where she'd been dancing with Crey and ran over, somehow managing not to trip on her layers of skirts.

They stared at each other for a second, then leaned together, Teresa hugging her as best she could around the sleeping Charlotte.

"I wish I could come," she said.

"I wish you would," Kate replied. "And I'm sorry that I can't stay. This place, it's not enough for me. I have to go back."

"I know." Teresa leaned down, and kissed Charlotte on the forehead. "I always knew you were the strong one, Kate. That you'd outgrow me."

"I couldn't," Kate forced out, refusing to cry. She'd gotten that out of her system already. "We're best friends, remember?"

"I'll try to reach you again." Teresa glanced back at the party. "If I can. If there's anything left. I'll try."

"I'll come," Kate promised.

She walked backward down the silver path, keeping Teresa in view. With each step, the party grew a little more distant, a little more indistinct, until all she could see was Teresa, standing alone in a ridiculous white gown.

And then she was standing in a fountain, in a midnight park, and Charlotte was stirring in her arms.

"Where'd everyone go?" she asked, words slurred with sleep.

"We're home, love." Kate braced herself, not sure how Charlotte would take the news.

"Oh."

Silence. Kate kept walking, not looking back at the moon and the fountain and the world they'd left behind.

But Charlotte, shifting to peer over her shoulder: "It's all gone."

"That's how it works."

"Can we visit again?"

At first, Kate's throat tightened. The old fear of doorways and forevers taking over. But then she looked back too, admiring the water, so silver in the moonlight, like the lakes Charlotte would never get to see.

"I hope so. I think Aunt Teresa would like it very much if we did."

"And you too?"

"And me too."

"Good." Charlotte yawned and nuzzled against Kate's chest. "Let's go home, Mommy."

Kate kissed her daughter's curls, then swung her down to stand. "Lead the way. My arms are getting tired."

After a few sleepy steps, Charlotte found her usual energy, and Kate let her run. The moon cast everything in silver, and Charlotte knew the way. There was nothing to be afraid of.

Kate looked back, one last time, smiling in case Teresa was watching. Then she turned and followed her daughter home.

*See Kelly Sandoval's story "The Otherside of Memory" online at Metaphorosis.*
*If you liked it, leave a comment. Authors love that!*
*Remember to subscribe to our e-mail updates so you'll know when new stories are posted.*

## About the story

I grew up on portal fantasies. I loved *The Labyrinth*, *The Chronicles of Narnia*, and *Peter Pan*. I wanted more than anything to disappear through a wardrobe, or a painting, and find myself somewhere else. Somewhere special.

But even as a kid, there were elements of the stories that bothered me. Especially Narnia. The characters live out their lives in this magical world. They're forced, as children, to fight. They grow up. They rule as kings and queens. And then they return to their lives and homes, magically children again. I could never believe that they would simply be fine with living as normal kids. I could hardly accept that they'd return in the first place.

The "Otherside of Memory" grew out of that tension. What does it mean to stay in a magical world, especially one that, as so many do, seems to exist as a reflection of its visitors? What does it take to leave it behind? And why would you?

In a way, this story is a conversation between the child me, who still longs for portals, and the current me, who sees the darker, more troubling side of such fantasies.

## A question for the author

**Q:** Are you an outline or discovery writer?

**A:** I'm mostly a discovery writer. I sit down with an idea and try to follow it. Lately though, I've been trying to teach myself to outline.

## About the author

Kelly lives in Seattle, where the weather is always happy to make staying in and writing seem like a good idea. She shares her home with her chaos tornado toddler, exhausted husband, and increasingly irate cat. Her interactive fiction is available from Choice of Games, where her current title is "Runt of the Litter".

www.kellysandovalfiction.com, @kellymsandoval

# A Universe All to Himself

Ryan Priest

Except death, this was the worst-case scenario. This was the inevitable cost of the space program. Given enough runs, this was going to happen to someone and you just prayed it wouldn't be you. The very mention of the possibility passed like a cold draft through the rec rooms or cafeterias of any space station. When a pilot failed to return from a mission, you hoped secretly, for their sake, that they were dead. The alternative was a man or woman hopelessly lost in space.

Erik Hale, Pilot #1225, had just won the lottery. Outside of his spaceship there was nothing; no star, no planet, no swirling black holes, not even the hollowed-out core of a dead gas giant. It was just cold, empty space.

His upper lip began to tremble.

The way *leaping* worked involved the compression of near-empty space. The astro-pilots called it the Planet-to-Planet Freeway. The computers charted a course between two planets orbiting in different star systems. Then the engines compressed the empty space between the two points. What was left? Usually only a few miles of concentrated space dust to cross and then your ship was there, at the other end, in a new solar system. The Leap window could only exist for a little over a second, and so a pilot had to circle the origin planet a couple of times to build up the speed to slingshot their ship fast enough to get out the other side before the window closed.

But you *had* to have a planet for the Leap back home. Without the planet's gravitational boost, the ship's propulsion could never build up the speed on its own. If you tried to use a star, the orbit would take too long; by the time you made it back around the ebb and tide of celestial movements would leave you pointing in the wrong direction. The planets, stars, galaxies were in a perpetual state of motion, like an ocean, never all in the exact same alignment twice.

The problem was that long-range telemetry could be unreliable. When analyzing celestial bodies tens of thousands of light years away, there was no way to be sure those planets would still be there on arrival. The computer analysts did their best to calculate good candidates; the brass wouldn't intentionally send you to a system that might have gone nova or to a planet with an orbit they weren't sure about.

Once arriving at their destination and landed, the astro-pilots collected data with their computers and sensors. Soil and air samples to check for human colony feasibility, astronomic readings to hunt for even more unknown planets, possibly so far out that they were undetectable from Earth. The pilot's final duty was to take a picture of his or herself holding the Western Earth Union flag. This was what really mattered to the brass. International space regulations required a live human being to physically be on the planet to establish ownership. The remaining nations of Earth were in a race to find and lay claim to inhabitable or resource rich exo-planets. Footprints and flags — the moon landing writ large across the galaxy.

With the job done, the pilot and ship reentered orbit and jumped back to their point of origin— for Westerners usually the Neptune or Pluto orbital stations.

But there *were* mistakes. When flying off into the universe in a blind rush, there was bound to be an error here or there. A black hole might have eaten the entire star, a collision with a comet might have destroyed the planet. No one would ever know for sure, because without the anchor planet, there was no way to establish a return trip to Earth. In the cases when a pilot did not come back, that destination was marked in the database as a 'No-Go'. There were no rescue missions. The only thing worse than losing an astronaut to space was losing a second astronaut sent to find out what happened to the first one.

Without the Leap Engine, a regular five-minute trip back to Earth from Pluto took over three years, even with their fastest engines. To get to the next closest exo-planet would take thousands of years. For a lost pilot — for Erik — there was no going home. Earth was gone and the Sun was only one of a million dots of light in the ship's portholes.

Erik was overcome with the desire to cry. He felt claustrophobic all of a sudden, and couldn't breathe. The safety harness squeezed his chest with every breath; it seemed alive and hostile, holding him to his seat, pinning him to this predicament. He felt as if all the blackness in the universe were closing in around him, suffocating him. He clawed at the restrictive harness in a panic, hoping he'd wake to find himself struggling with a sheet wrapped around his neck. But this was no dream. He was trapped; the universe had trapped him out here alone and his mother wasn't going to flip on the lights and make it all okay. His mother was gone, now and forever. She'd be told he was dead and she'd collapse into his sister's arms and they'd weep together. But then they and the world would ultimately learn to go on without him. His entire life was now separated from him by an unimaginable and uncrossable ocean of black nothingness.

"What if it *does* happen?" trainees always asked when first confronted with the possibility of a failed jump.

"It won't happen. But if it does, then press this button. That's all for now," the trainer would say, and shuffle them on to the next lesson. Every ship had a button, a red one hidden out of view, near the floor and covered by a black latch so no one ever had to think about it.

What did the button do? People seldom spoke about it openly, but you'd hear things; there were theories. Some said it released a pistol or maybe some suicide pills for the pilot to take. The old space freighter captains claimed that a hundred years ago, when transit around the solar system was still new and could take years, the old timers all had such pills aboard for worst-case scenarios. Back when if something happened to your ship, you were months or possibly years away from rescue. Erik could do months, he could even do years, but *never* was a different hell altogether. The pills had been a quicker and supposedly less painful death than freezing, roasting, suffocating, or any of the other ways a botched space flight might end you. Supposedly.

Others thought the button was a self-destruct for the entire ship. They said it was designed that way so you wouldn't know you were killing yourself. Proponents of this theory said it was for the religious minded who might fear that suicide would damage their chances of a pleasurable afterlife. You could press the button as many times as you liked, but it was programmed not to engage unless the ship missed its departure window.

One pilot, #108 Sheila Gates, after arriving, had found her host planet's sun moved in-between her anchor planet and Earth. She'd been forced to wait for the planet to orbit back around the other side, four and a half Earth years. When her ship *did* return, Sheila was inside, alive but catatonic. Other pilots said that she had been locked up in a room somewhere in the Department of Space. Rumor was that she'd pressed the red button.

He looked at the black cover for a moment or two. It was as if opening the latch and seeing the red button underneath would make this all permanent. If he did it, then he was admitting that a real disaster had happened.

"Think Erik, think!" His voice cracked and he found the simple task of focusing on anything beyond his grasp. This was bad, this was *very* bad.

"Why would you want to fly off to plant flags on planets you'll never see again?" his old friend Benny's voice ran through his memory. They'd been co-captains on a space-freighter that hauled minerals from asteroid mining sites to giant space platforms.

At the time, Erik had kept his motivations personal and shrugged him off with, "Hey, after two hundred jumps and with some smart investing you can retire to a comfortable life."

Benny was a couple years older, had more hours in space. For him, the gift of steady work was all that he ever wanted. To Erik freight hauling had only ever been a means to collect the flight time needed to apply to be an astro-pilot in the Department of Space, and once he had them he was gone. He'd really liked Benny, but growing up, Erik had had three different stepdads and more "mom's boyfriends" than he could count. He was used to saying goodbye to older men.

Now, facing catastrophic loss, he was asking himself the same question. Why *had* he done this to himself? Did he really think it mattered in the grand scheme of things that in two or three hundred years there would be children growing up on faraway colonies, learning in school that he'd discovered their planet? Maybe even a planet named after him? In his one hundred and fifty-seven jumps, he had found seven inhabitable exo-planets. Seven new worlds where everyone would know the name starship pilot #1225 Erik Hale and the subsequent endnote, that he was lost in space.

Hours later, and his eyes were still locked on the round, red knob on his floor. Maybe death, maybe insanity, maybe salvation — but what other choice did he have?

He prepared himself to die. He took a deep breath of sterile air, enough to carry his spirit into eternity, as Ernie, one of his mother's many boyfriends, had explained. Ernie had worn an old Native American jacket and vintage tie-dyed shirts. He liked to talk about spirituality and that sort of thing. This had been Erik's only exposure to any type of religion and it, along with his mother's relationship with Ernie, had been brief.

It amazed him what chose to pop into his mind at this, potentially last, moment. He latched on to that amazement — not a bad feeling to go out on — and exhaled as he let his hand press down on the button...

No explosion, no afterlife, no death. He was still lost and alone, yet his life seemed to taste a little sweeter. Two small, blue pills had ejected from behind the button like a coin-operated candy dispenser, and the computer screens in the cockpit had all gone blank. Erik picked the pills up off the floor. They were ovular, like vitamins, but he knew they weren't vitamins. They were the opposite.

Suicide pills. Erik looked at them in disappointment. A second ago, before pressing the button, he might not have cared, but now he was very sure that he wanted to live.

"So, your ship has been lost in space," came a familiar voice out of the ship's speakers. He couldn't place it at first, but when all the monitors faded in with an accompanying video, he recognized the face immediately. It was H. Gregory

Gladstone, Secretary of Space and Exploration. "The first thing you must remember is not to panic. Take a deep breath."

Erik complied. Trying to calm down, he realized just how tightly wound he'd become. The muscles in his neck and shoulders felt carved in stone and he had a clenched mouthful of gritting teeth. He closed his eyes and took three deep, measured, breaths. On the final exhale, he let his eyes open. It was better; things were somewhat clearer.

"In your hand are two blue tablets. If you take them, death will be quick. However, you have also been given a key that unlocks a special box on this ship. Should you choose to use it, this box contains the means not only to your survival, but also your sanity. More importantly, in this box you will find the tools necessary to regain what you've lost, a meaningful life, love, friendship. It will require an incredible amount of work, but I promise you, should you choose, there is still a life for you to have."

Erik looked down and saw that a brass key had also been ejected from the emergency latch. He picked it up, and held the key in his left hand and the suicide tablets in his right.

"Take a moment." Gladstone's face was calming. He'd been a public figure for over forty years and had been one of the lead designers of the Leap system. He'd managed to keep himself above all the political fray and stand out as someone for the intellectuals to follow and support. He had no agenda other than the continued exploration and eventual colonization of space. That was his brand and it came with a good public reputation. He was like a family member, only one who lived entirely on television and whose interactions were completely one-sided. Still, Erik had always rooted for his success and supported anything he did.

"In seven minutes, your tablets will dissolve and become useless to you. Sorry for putting you on the spot, but you pressed the button, which tells me you are ready to move ahead, either in one way or the other. It is time for decisive action. The choice you make now must stand. You will either decide that you want to live and are willing to put forth the work and sacrifice that is necessary, or you will die now and commit yourself to a different journey."

At that, Gladstone quit speaking but continued to stand there, looking into the camera, lest you be completely alone in your final moments. There was no judgment implied in his tone. Erik wondered how many other pilots had watched this video, made this choice. It was generally assumed that if a pilot didn't make it back, they were dead, but who could know for sure?

He fought back sobs. How had he put himself in this position? He didn't need a planet named after him. That all seemed like such an arrogant conceit at this point; barely more than celestial graffiti. Now he had H. Gregory Gladstone telling him he might just want to kill himself and be done with it?

He looked down at the pills and instantly pictured himself foaming at the mouth, twitching and swallowing his own tongue. He dropped the pills to the floor as if they were on fire. They'd already begun to crumble and, in a few minutes, they'd be nothing but inert microscopic dust.

This was it. Whatever lay ahead, this was his life and he would try his best to make the most of it and hope that the

Secretary of Space really did have some ace up his sleeve.

Gladstone suddenly came back to life. "If you are still listening to this, then that means the pills are gone and you are alive. I am proud of you for making such a difficult decision in this, such an uncertain time. But rest assured, the road to your new life begins now."

Erik was directed to the rear of the ship, in the already cramped storage area. He saw that a new box was waiting for him on the floor, recently ejected from a hidden compartment. He felt a delicate beat of hope rise within him. There was more to this puzzle. Director Gladstone *did* have a plan for him.

With the brass key still clutched in the fingers of his left hand, he approached the box and, sure enough, there was a lock waiting for him to open it. All the pageantry was likely for psychological effect. Here was a box that he knew no pilot outside of his situation had ever seen. This box was truly a mystery and every possibility in the universe could very well be inside.

He ran his fingers over the top of it lightly, the same way he always did with a new ship. This was what was going to get him home. The box itself was maybe three by four feet and not very high off the ground, about the size of a great chest.

He turned the lock and took the lid off. Hand-tools, spare nuts and bolts, bags of soil, and several packets of seeds. At the very bottom was one more object, a small package whose label read: Protocol 6, Final Phase. Do Not Open Early.

He was careful to not even touch the Protocol 6 package. He would follow the rules; this was too important to screw up with impatience. The seeds were indication enough that whatever this was, it was going to take time.

A new program came up on his console. Protocol One. It was a series of instructions, laid out in precise steps. The first were on how to set up a garden and to expand the ship's insides to allow for as much space for movement as possible. The garden was the most important part. The garden would filter and recycle the air and someday take the place of his mission packs when it came to food.

Sixteen hours a day. That was how much the program kept him working. When the day was over, he'd lie down while a monotone, pre-programmed voice continued to talk to him, encouraging him and telling him that it was hard now because these things had to get taken care of first, but the voice promised, it *promised*, there was something much better waiting for him if he followed the instructions step by step.

An alarm woke him up every morning. The voice urged him to brush his teeth, clean himself appropriately, and eat a protein bar. It always seemed to rush him along more quickly than he'd like, but he was usually too tired to care. Those first few days were about nothing but toil, every single day, morning, noon, and night, which meant absolutely nothing here in black space.

He hardly had any time to think about how his mother might be taking the news. No time to picture his own funeral back home and imagine the eulogy his sister Andrea might have given for him. Would anybody else even be there? He hadn't seen Benny in years. Ernie and all the stepdads were long gone.

The thought of an empty funeral was a reminder that he'd failed to accomplish anything or make a positive impact on anyone's life, though he'd wanted to. But like everything else, friendships had been pushed to the back burner in favor of that mad rush to pull himself out of the working class. In a moment of bitter irony, the life back home that had never been good enough for him had now been taken from him.

The ship was designed so that once he emptied out an interior panel's shelves and drawers, the walls could be folded outward, expanding like origami. When completed, he'd have more than triple the space. Awkward and unflightworthy, he'd never be able to land the ship on a planet again, but that didn't matter; there wasn't another planet for a million miles.

"Moving on to Protocol 2." The program's voice droned on with instructions and random encouragements. "You're doing a fantastic job. You're almost there."

He began to realize the program wasn't just teaching him how to reorganize his ship, the program was designed to slowly but surely reorganize *him.*

This meant that someone had thought this through. Someone had done tests and planned for this, and they knew how best to survive the loss of, basically, everything he'd ever known. He took wry comfort in this, imagining a room full of college boys with all the answers planning out his every little move.

The nightly talk downs became more than just encouragement. As he sat on the cockpit chair, eating his dinner, the ship's voice would ask him weighty questions and give him puzzles to think about over the next day. The questions ranged from the unanswerable koans — "If a tree falls in the forest..." — to highly complex exercises in logic — "If Archbishop Thomas needs a census of a kingdom containing ten villages, and he knows each village has ten more persons than the last, that no village has more than three hundred people and no village has less than two hundred, how many people total live in the kingdom?"

The program did not shy away from sharing its motivations. It was trying to strengthen his mind. Something really great was apparently coming down the line and having a quick and strong mind that could think things through was a prerequisite.

After two weeks, the expansion work was completed. He had his space home. The cockpit, the garden in the left aft of the cargo hold, the right side set up with his bed and personal effects. It wasn't much at all, really, but it was much more than he'd had or expected when he started. That was the program, to make things better in small increments, keep him working for more, keep him busy. They were breaking him down, like basic training or a cult.

With Protocol 3, the computer led him through nightly, guided meditations. He was asked to picture simple objects, a beach ball or log cabin. Through a series of open-ended questions, the computer made him fixate on the mental image, flesh it out.

"What color is the cabin? Do the insides contain an odor? If so, do you like this odor? Why?"

At the end of the lessons and throughout the day, the computer would periodically remind him that something great was coming, that he was almost ready. Almost.

Coming from genetically modified seeds, the plants were growing big and fast. With only the smallest amount of maintenance, he would begin producing his own food within a few weeks. The computers rewarded him with music while he worked, and even allowed the viewing of a film every so often. There was no way to tell how many hours of footage had been stored in the memory banks. It was inevitable, though, that one day he'd have run out of videos and have listened to every song. The program was designed to push that day as far into the future as possible.

By Protocol 4, he'd begun to notice results from all of his exercises. He was becoming mentally sharper. He was solving puzzles more easily, thinking through the koans more deeply.

What was Protocol 6 and how did it figure into all of this? Had there been a breakthrough in cognitive sciences? For years, people had been claiming the next wave of human evolution would see an increase in mental powers — telepathy, maybe. Would he become able to contact Earth and tell them to find a way to send a rescue? Was it even possible that they had a way to master telekinesis? Maybe he'd unlock some as of yet unused part of his brain and be able to move his spaceship across light years with just a thought. Anything was possible, and the program kept promising it'd lead to a life worth living. It promised an escape from this cell which, as it stood, would one day double as his tomb.

The meditations became even more involved. Now it wasn't just log cabins. He was being asked to see whole landscapes, to hold the image in his head so long that he could account for every little blip on the horizon. The landscapes became increasingly involved. Erik always followed along. He asked himself the questions he was supposed to and he tried his best to come up with the answers. He did this in total earnestness, as with everything else. The Space Department's motto was *Cynicism Kills*.

He'd always been good at following orders. He knew that about himself but wasn't sure how he felt about it. With nothing but time on his hands and these sharper mental tools, he realized that he wasn't weak or inherently obedient, he simply longed for a sense of fatherly approval. He was always trying to show the world that he could follow directions, that he was worthwhile, and that someone would realize this and take him under their wing to teach him how to navigate this confusing life as a man. *That* confusing life. He had to remind himself that his old world and any hang-ups that went with it were a thing of the past.

Erik had pushed forward, full force, the very picture of pluck and vinegar. He was no stranger to hard work. Hard work was how he'd pulled himself off the surface and into space. How he'd become a pilot and had eventually made it to astro-pilot. He recognized that effort multiplied by time inevitably led to results. He'd learned to subvert the part of himself that wanted to laze, to sit back and think of reasons *not* to bother. The voice in the background of every endeavor that whispered maledictions about fruitlessness, failure and abdication.

But the days turned into weeks, the routine became rigmarole, and try as hard as he might to tune it out, the voice of negativity in his head had grown louder. His situation was beginning to wear on him. Forcing optimism became more difficult with each passing day.

He missed home and he missed other people. Anyone. He missed mattering in someone else's life or even the possibility of affecting another person. Nothing he did here, nothing he would ever say or think could ever be known by another living person. He was effectively a ghost, living without the possibility of consequence, and this was a realization that, once registered, could not so easily be broken free from.

"Do not give up," the program chirped through the speakers. And he tried, he tried, to hold out hope. He practiced his exercises, but mustering the required energy was becoming an effort. He felt that he was growing weaker and not stronger. He began thinking up his own dark koans. "If a man exists without consequence, is he even alive?"

His hopes for Protocol 6 began to fade as well. If there was telekinesis or telepathy, why hadn't they already used it to make contact with *him*? He began to suspect more and more that Protocol 6 was going to be a new set of suicide pills. There was no escape from this place.

Protocol 5.

"Prepare to meditate, Erik." The computer was programmed to use his first name. It was just a series of 1s and 0s, with no humanity. "Tonight, you will think of a house. Not just any house; imagine your perfect house. This is the house you would most like to live in."

It went on asking him to furnish this house. Did it have a pool? What was the climate like? This meditation went further and longer than all others before it. So much so that he actually began to find it taxing and, by the end of the lesson, had developed quite a little headache.

Every night the following week, the program immediately would tell him to concentrate on the house he'd created. He was told to imagine himself walking through the house. Going into each room, opening every closet.

"When your hand touches the wood, how does it feel? What do you see when you look out the window?" Oak, or at least what he imagined oak to be. It felt cool and smooth, it felt like money. Outside of his window were rolling green hills, a shimmering sea bay, backdropped by an impossibly bright, blue sky, sprinkled with cotton ball clouds. Every night, he made the house just a little more beautiful, just a little more *him*. He noticed that the more he did this, the less strain it caused. This, he actually felt he was getting better at. His brain was learning this imaginary house.

After this, every meditation began with the house and then expanded from there. He was told to walk down the street. It was like a game. He was sent exploring outside of this house. He could go anywhere he wanted, but there were rules. He couldn't just imagine a restaurant and place himself there. He had to consciously walk down the street, see the restaurant in the distance and step by step approach it. He could have anything he wanted, and do anything, but there were no shortcuts.

The game became fun again as it challenged him more and more every day. He'd built an entire town in his head, and without fail could recall all of the details as clearly as the Akron suburbs he'd passed through as a child, longing for one of those lives with lawns and playgrounds. Only this was better, cleaner, greener, and brighter.

The game was the high point of his day. Any time spent concentrating on the game was time not spent in the downward spiral of hopelessness and loneliness.

"What is a town without people? Who lives nearest to you on the West? A man, a woman, a family?" The computer had him not only build people but build his past relationships with them. How had they met? Did he like them?

Erik's imagined house sat directly east of a family named the Woodneys, a name he'd been asked to imagine on the spot, without any reference to anyone he really knew. The Woodneys were Tom and Cheryl, and they had one son, Zach, who was ten.

Where the game became really interesting started on a movie night. He'd been allowed to watch an old movie from the Nineteen-Nineties. Normal enough, but later that night, in meditation, he was asked to enter his fake house, in his fake town, and go to visit his fake neighbor Tom. By now, Erik had been asked so many questions by the program, he would be just about able to write a thousand-word biography of Tom Woodney.

However, tonight the program did something different. "You see your neighbor in the yard. He tells you that he just saw the same movie. He really liked it. Discuss the movie with him. What did he find different about the movie, if anything, than you did?"

And he found that this was a very easy and fun conversation to have. Tom's words came out naturally, by necessity of his personality.

Before he knew it, the two-hour meditation session was over and he was called to return his attention to the ship and its clutter of blooming plants.

It was only when he was allowed another movie that he realized what the program was doing. He was watching some god-awful thriller from the Twenty-Naughts. Erik hated the movie, but he found himself excited to see what neighbor Tom would have to say about it.

That night he had another two-hour movie conversation with Tom while sitting outside around his dream house's crystal blue pool. This mental game the program had him playing not only passed the time but was also enjoyable.

To his further delight, the program took away his time limits. As long as he followed the other rules, he could play the game as late as he wanted.

The last step before Protocol 6 was to keep the game going during his day. Periodically throughout the day, at different times, the computer would ask him to check on the game and see what was happening. He closed his eyes and then he was there, walking along the side of a lake, or shopping.

The program explained that Protocol 6 would be unlocked when he was able to go into the game while continuing to do his chores, mind his garden, perform the ship's required maintenance. Access to Protocol 6 was on the honor system. A new option in the ship's control panel read: PROTOCOL 6 and he could access it anytime, but like the little package bearing the same name, he'd been warned not to skip ahead, not to cheat. To make sure Protocol 6 worked, he had to be one hundred percent.

So the game went on. He tested himself — at one minute he'd be clipping some tomatoes, while simultaneously in the game he'd be playing second base on the local softball team he'd dreamt up. His directive had been to choose a sport, organize a league, and join a team.

He no longer even needed to close his eyes to be in the game and see everything in high definition. Just to be sure, he waited a while, until there was no question, until he spent more time in the game than he did out of it. He could water the plants and check the systems in fifteen minutes, then the lights would go off and he'd float in total darkness playing the game. By this time, he had a pretty good idea of what Protocol 6 would entail. He assumed it was designed that way.

He was ready. He sat in his cockpit chair and selected Protocol 6. The anxiousness in his gut was palpable. All this time he'd waited, he'd worked himself to the bone and he'd waited even more, and now here it was, Protocol 6.

All the screens in the ship went blank momentarily and a familiar face dissolved into view. It was H. Gregory Gladstone again. "First, I'd like to tell you how proud we all are of you for making it this far. You are a testament to the true indomitability of the human spirit. Next, let me get this over with quickly. You are not going home."

Inside, he had known that he wasn't going to make it home, but still, the final confirmation came like a knife to his heart. Hope died hard.

"That being said, do not give up. I'm sure by now you must what realize what Protocol 6 is."

"The game." Erik responded, knowing that Gladstone couldn't hear him. This message had been recorded years ago. All of it had, before he ever joined the space program.

"The game *is* your salvation. If you have done your exercises, then the world you've created in the game should have become, at times, just as real to you as the world of your spaceship. Here is the secret. It *is* just as real. Continue to play the game, give it your all, and you will be able to find fulfillment inside." Gladstone looked solemn, his bushy, serious eyes reminding Erik that cynicism killed.

It was a lot that they were asking of him, but really there was no choice. The program had not lied. There was no way he could have played the game, not at such a high level, without the slow and steady buildup of cognitive training.

The game was his favorite thing. It occupied his thoughts, it was the source of his happiness, his humor. The people he met in the game now seemed just as authentic to him as real people in the real world.

There wasn't any choice to quit playing. The game was as much a part of him now as his arm. What Gladstone was asking him to do was to go all in, to accept the game as reality.

"There is no difference to your mind if something is real or imagined. What makes dreams less important than reality is that we forget them and that they have no bearing on our future. Nevertheless, when we go to sleep and dream, no matter how fanciful that dream world, no matter how little sense it makes, still we accept it as reality without a second thought. Now you may open the final package."

Erik took the small parcel from the floor and opened it. Inside were two items, their purpose immediately recognizable to him. A simple switch system for automated plant watering and a feeding tube.

"The rules of time and space no longer need apply in the game. You'll find you can make time pass more quickly or more slowly. No reason to limit yourself to the ticks of seconds taken from Earth-based clocks. Now that the game is truly yours, make the very most of it."

By now he loved Gladstone like a father. He'd had no one else since being marooned, but he knew this was the last time he would ever see him.

Gladstone's final message was, "When you are ready, press continue." And with that, his image faded back out into the world of the left behind. A big green button on the screen replaced him, bearing the label: Continue.

It had to be this way. There was no going back, there had never been any going back. Everything ahead lay in the game, a new life completely untethered from his previous existence. He began to make his preparations. His movements were slow and deliberate. He was cognizant that this was a turning point in his life. The end of one thing and the beginning of something entirely different.

He set up his plant feeders, double-checked the cycles, automated his food and waste processing. When he was finished, everything was set up to run on complete automation. At last, he sat down in front of the console and choked down one end of the feeding tube, which connected itself to the ready supply of processed food paste from his garden.

When finished and ready, Erik lifted from his chair until he was free floating, the cabin lit only by the soft glow of the green button. He pressed Continue. Everything went black. The monotone voice of the program came back online and swam through the air.

"Erik, prepare to mediate. You are in your house. You hear a knock at the front door. You open it. It's a woman. She's the most beautiful woman you've ever seen. What color is her hair? What about her eyes? You like the way she smells, the way her voice sounds as she tells you, 'Hello, I just moved into the area.' What is her name?"

"Betty…" Erik said to himself while at the same time smiling at Betty and inviting her in for a cup of coffee. This was it. There'd be no more instructions.

The ship continued to float off into the cosmos, on its way to nowhere, a million miles away from where it started. Erik continued too, expanding his world. He married Betty, they had children. He loved them and knew that they loved him.

He found that time *could* pass faster in the game, living years in the space of months, full lifetimes in the course of years. He had evolved. He now existed as something different than a man. He had anything and everything he wanted. His existence was a beating pulse of a thousand different points of view in a world that continued forward with its own set of rules. He no longer cared if he had a planet named after him somewhere. He was now an entire universe unto himself.

*See Ryan Priest's story "A Universe All to Himself" online at Metaphorosis.*
*If you liked it, leave a comment. Authors love that!*
*Remember to subscribe to our e-mail updates so you'll know when new stories are posted.*

## About the story

I grew up all over the Southwest. Colorado, Texas, California, the former frontier lands. When staring out at the Great Plains or the vast Rocky Mountains I often think of the people from the past. The catastrophic loneliness of a frontiersman or a scout. There will be new frontiers in our future and new explorers needed to map them. We will get brand new types of heroes, flying through space and maybe even dimensions we haven't discovered yet. This story tries to examine both.

I was inspired by the stories of gold-hungry miners, ex-slaves still looking for their freedom, lone Native Americans without a tribe wandering through a seemingly endless wilderness with nothing but their thoughts and their iron will to keep them company. What makes that type of will? Is it something we're either born with or an ability that develops after trial and tribulation? Willpower, when used effectively, has created the greatest feats of mankind. Where else might it take us?

Where are we going as a species? Are we going to reach other planets and is it just planets all the way down to the end of time or will we learn to take on new dimensions, new modalities of thought? What will a 'day' mean when there's no Sun to rotate around? We can never go back to the days of the past. There is only the future for us, and the beautiful thing about the future is, anything can happen.

## A question for the author

**Q:** Have you ever consciously written a 'message' story? Was it easier or harder than usual?

**A:** One of my favorite aspects of writing is the serendipity of a story developing a message or deeper meaning while in the process of writing. Even when started from a blank page, a story will develop its own ideas. Now, when you flip it, choose the message before the story, it can be a very difficult task to get right. I've had to rewrite a story from the ground up three or four times when going in with a prescribed message. Sometimes the telling, no matter how good, doesn't lend itself to the desired ideal. When finally you do chart the trail that leads to the correct message, delivered in just the right way, that is a magic all its own. It's calling order out of chaos and it's beautiful.

## About the author

Ryan Priest escaped the pollution-covered palm trees of L.A. for the mountain evergreens just outside Denver. He is a Black American who loves freedom, irresponsibility, and every single moment in history where a human being has let go and just gone for it in attempt to create something amazing.

www.RyanPriest.net, @Ryan_Priest

# Autumn's Come Undone

Sharmon Gazaway

Autumn stands before a large pumpkin. Her bare soles, planted on either side, draw up minerals from the rich loam. The pumpkin's skin, still warm in late afternoon, glows under her touch, deepening from apricot to bittersweet orange. Stepping to the next pumpkin, she works the row, ripening each in turn. She swipes her brow with her forearm, her hands grimy, and pulls the weight of her ginger hair off her hot neck. A murmuring rumples the treetops, whispers forming words she can't quite make out. A chill lifts the fine hairs on her nape and she shivers.

Probably those air-headed dryads gossiping again.

As she walks to the brook to wash, honey-bright leaves drift down, cling to her hair like sprites. Humming, she pirouettes, her leaf skirts a swirl of marigold, russet, and spice. A garland of purplish-green globes dangling from the branch of a hickory tree catches her eye. She breaks off the vine and holds it up to the fading light.

Crow flutters down to the lowest limb, his bent wing stiff.

"Muscadines," she calls to him. "Sol's favorite." She breathes on the globes and they take on a ruddier, sweeter hue. "Perfect."

She drapes the fruited vine across a low shrub on the brook's bank and kneels, scrubbing her hands in the icy water. The stream babbles up at her, unintelligible at first. Dryads flit across the brook, tittering, cover malicious smiles with hazy hands. She looks about, wondering where Sylvannah is and why she hasn't already herded them into their trees. She swishes the muscadine vine through the water, shaking her head. It's a mystery to her how she ever endured the flighty things before Sylvannah came.

Crow lights on her shoulder, nudging her head. She shrugs him onto the bank. So little time left to prepare the table for Sol's visit tomorrow, and the muscadines will be the finishing touch. The stream murmurs insistently and Crow tilts his head toward it, turns and looks up at Autumn. She leans down, listens carefully. The murmurs sharpen into words that glint and wound, and take her breath.

Rising, the soggy fruit slides from her slack fingers.

Autumn's leaf skirts rush and crackle as she stumbles through the darkening woods, throws herself beneath the arms of the Great Oak. She hooks her fingers in deep, harrows leaf-rot and worm castings, breaks her nails on the bones of birds and vermin. From low in her inner turnings a cry germinates, a cry that, breaking free, rattles branches and drives the dryads into their tree-skins.

She does not cry prettily. Not like Spring, who mastered the art of the one perfect dewdrop tear while they were still girls in Earth's nursery.

Moaning, Autumn rolls her head on the forest floor and grits her teeth, the moss clinging to her lips. She hears a crack inside her chest like the snap of a twig.

Pushing onto her hands and knees, she crawls closer to the Oak. She huddles between the roots, her back pressed against the furrowed trunk. She curls into her cloak, fastens its silver acorn brooch, and tucks in her bare feet, tight as Tortoise in his shell. Crow lights on her shoulder and roosts in her tangles. Autumn presses her wet cheek against moonshadowed bark, relieved Sol can't see her now.

All night she burns, shamed.

Like a fool, all day she hummed and danced while she worked, awaiting Sol's visit. In a large reed basket, she heaped the harvest's bounty—rosy apples, pomegranates, walnuts and pecans, lush persimmons. She set it on a table strewn with smilax vines by the brook. She savored the thought of Sol by her side for a whole day, wandering the meadow amongst violet and ochre wildflowers, drifting in a rowboat until moonset.

She presses cold fingers against her blazing cheeks.

When morning comes, newly resurrected and only half alive, it sheds its mists and feeds on shafts of light. Light that colors everything the soft gold of Sol's hair. It fingers her face with tender warmth. She knows this touch—*his* touch—intimately.

Sol is mocking her.

She shudders to her feet, sends Crow flapping. She slaps twigs from her cloak, squares her shoulders and pulls up her hood, shielding herself from Sol's gloating.

This is not to be borne.

She marches to the brook, and heaves the table over. The loaded basket crashes to the ground, the fruit bruised and bleeding. She strikes her hands together and sparks shoot from her fingertips. The basket erupts in flame.

Shaking, rage unspent, she sets her face to the North and trudges out of her wood. Crow clings to her gray woolen shoulder, weight-shifting nervously. Mice dart for cover at her approach.

Whisking into vapor, Sylvannah slipped out through a knothole in the Great Oak when the wailing and gnashing of teeth began. All the other dryads shivered inside their trees. But she bit her lip and witnessed Autumn unravel.

Now, with Sol high in the eastern sky, and Autumn and Crow gone, the dryads' gossip chitters tree to tree.

"Sol jilted Autumn, even though she's never loved another."

"I heard he cheated on her with a star."

"No, two stars."

"They say he actually expects her to be happy for him."

Sylvannah listens, amused. Sol doesn't know Autumn the way she does, if that's what he expects. She snorts. As if.

It was Autumn's silly sister, Spring, who else? A bigger flirt she never saw. Sylvannah began life in Spring's woodland where Spring was forever tempting this star and that to come down to her. And when they burned out on the way, her eyes, the yellow-green of a cat's, glittered. She clapped as they blazed and fell to cinders at her feet.

And now she's caught the biggest star of all.

Sylvannah shushes the dryads, and glides into the orchard. She simply can't see the attraction. Sol is larger than life, always seeking attention. Yes, yes his job is very important—but, nutshells, what a Golden Boy.

Autumn gave him her heart long ago. Sylvannah couldn't imagine a better match for Autumn. Fiery; everyone around her gets singed at some point. But Sol could handle it, even seemed to revel in her volatile nature.

True, Autumn is unpredictable, but she has a warm and generous spirit few in the wood ever see.

Sylvannah remembers the day many harvests ago when she discovered Autumn's forest. She watched from the cover of a pine thicket as Autumn tended to an injured bird.

"Stop skulking around the edges of the wood and introduce yourself," Autumn called to her that day, tying the bird's wing firmly with strips of linen.

Sylvannah glided out, one hand clinging to chunky bark.

Autumn glanced up and sighed, "Not another dryad." She ran her hand over the crow's ragged feathers. "So, what do you want?"

"I'm Sylvannah. I come from Spring's woodland. She—she banished me."

Autumn looked up sharply. "Why?"

"I suppose your sister didn't much like me telling her she was cruel, the way she taunted the stars to their destruction." She shrugged.

Autumn smiled tightly, tossed her head toward the Oak in the center of the wood. "You're welcome to live there. You're the first dryad I've met with some sense and grit. If you can keep those nosy airheads out of my hair, you have a home for life."

So Sylvannah did.

Autumn kept to herself, except for Crow, her constant companion since she saved him from a hunter's snare. On occasion she visited her favorite sister, Winter. But she sought out Sol more than any other, the way a wing seeks wind.

Sylvannah accepts this. All she needs is the shelter of the Great Oak, his rings of wisdom surrounding her, his constancy —home.

And bossing the other dryads is just gravy.

She weaves through the orchard, inhales the brewery scent of apples that ache for Autumn's harvesting. Among shriveled, snaking vines, pumpkins bulge to bursting. The trees breathe the colors of fire.

As Sylvannah glides back toward the Oak, her lower lip sucked between her teeth, apprehension curls inside her like a little fog.

Autumn's sister, Winter, folds her into fur-robed arms and Autumn soaks up her warmth. Sol is weaker here. He and Winter have always maintained a distant relationship.

"I know why you've come, Little Acorn," Winter murmurs into her hair. "But Summer will never agree to it." She frowns, her eyes black and liquid as a snowhare's.

Summer. The good sister who tries to bind them together. But she has a soft spot for Sol, friends since the Beginning. She will plead for them all to reconcile, be a family. Family! Accept Sol as a *brother*?

"Sister," Autumn snaps, flaring, "I didn't come to ask a favor. Or permission." She sees in Winter's eye the glint of indulgent pride her sister reserves for Autumn alone. It was Winter who comforted her when Mother left them like fledglings in an abandoned nest. Winter who endured her tantrums, taught her to dance like a dervish to burn off the fumes of resentment. "I came to give," she adds softly.

Winter takes her hands in hers and studies the black-rimmed broken nails. "Autumn, you're overwrought. With good reason. What Sol did—"

"What *they* did," Autumn grinds out.

"Yes. They. But with time—"

"Time? Time will only multiply the pain. The humiliation. There is no one else for me. Ever."

Winter drops her hands. "Still. I can't agree to this." Her pallid brow creases. "What of duty? Those who depend on you?" Her eyes harden like jet. "I will not take your silver acorn."

"When the time comes, you must." Autumn juts her chin. "I have no one else."

Sparks and ice splinters fly between them. Winter reasons, then pleads. Autumn will not be moved.

Winter, her lips trembling, swallows hard, and agrees.

With Winter's white realm far behind her, Autumn stalks through her own forest to the Great Oak, jaw hard. Snails—too slow to escape—crunch beneath her feet. Her skirts now blaze full-blown maize-gold, cayenne, bittersweet—mushrooms ride her hem like mum death-bells.

"Sylvannah," Autumn calls, gently stroking Crow's crooked wing.

Sylvannah floats down hesitantly from a branch high in the Oak, wavering before her.

"I'm giving my silver acorn to my sister. Winter will know what to do."

"What," Sylvannah rasps, suddenly still as lichen on bark, "have you done?"

Autumn kneads Crow's silky head, smears tears off her face. She takes a shuddering breath and shakes him off. He reels twice, then perches in the Oak, head cocked.

"You might want to glide to the highest branches," Autumn says softly to Sylvannah.

Eyes closed, Autumn imagines Spring, beribboned and blushing in Sol's light, melting into him—as she herself longs to do, still.

She begins to twirl, her feet an axis, her skirts whirring like a swarm of locusts. She spins, faster. Visceral heat surges up from her core, charges her fingertips, sparks fly. She hurls fingerling flames scattershot. One by one the trees ignite, sacrificed on the pyre of her rage. The gold and wine of a hundred sunsets combust. Oak, maple, and pine pop and hiss their indignation—the screeching dryads flee.

Her skirts explode in a pentecost of wildfire. And she twirls.

At last, the pain exceeds the one in her cracked heart.

Sylvannah drifts through the charred ruins, smoke permeating her gossamer heart. At least the other dryads are safe with their cousins in the river where she drove them. Crow crouches atop an armless black pine, head hidden under his bent wing.

She managed to save the Great Oak, whisking the flames away from his vulnerable upper branches. She caresses his gnarled, ancient bark. Below, something glints in the ash. Swooping down, she retrieves the silver acorn clasp, icon of Autumn's power, for safekeeping.

And beneath it lies a smoldering, cracked acorn. Autumn's heart. This, she plants.

Winter comes to bury Autumn's ashes in mounds of pure white, as she promised.

Sylvannah fastens the silver acorn on Winter's furs, then glides up into the Oak's sturdiest branches and waits.

With Autumn's power, Winter is twice as strong. In time, Sol grows weak. Spring languishes, a pale shadow.

And Winter reigns. Some call it The Little Ice Age. Others call this particularly bitter time The Year Without a Summer.

Sylvannah calls it a reckoning.

*See Sharmon Gazaway's story "Autumn's Come Undone" online at Metaphorosis.*
*If you liked it, leave a comment. Authors love that!*
*Remember to subscribe to our e-mail updates so you'll know when new stories are posted.*

## About the story

"Autumn's Come Undone" began as a poem, a pantoum. I'd always wanted to write about a season personified. I had been focusing on poetry and wanted to get back to stories, so I thought this poem could be expanded. I'd also been reading about dryads and they somehow strayed into Autumn's story. My original poem image of Autumn was much darker. She had black hair and teetered over the edge of madness. She evolved into a fiery redhead, but kept that underlying hint of madness—a break with rational thought. I wanted to explore a character who gives herself over fully to her emotions and the passion of the moment, and discover what the cost and aftermath might look like.

## A question for the author

**Q:** What is your favorite word?

**A:** That's a tough one. If I'm going on the meaning of words, I guess it would have to be love, since there is no point to life without it. But I have a deep affection for the English language, love words for their sound and feel in the mouth. Words that sound like what they mean, such as undulate, haunting, sassy, poignant, and vicious are favorites. Poetically invented words like one I used in my story, moonshadowed, are always fun. I like ugly words that fit just right too, like muck or gutta-percha. Right now corvid (not to be confused with Covid!) is probably my favorite—I've written a string of poems, a short, and a flash on crows and birds of the corvid family.

## About the author

Sharmon Gazaway was born and raised in the deep south surrounded by Appalachia, obvious to anyone who hears her speak for more than a minute. She used to watch her Mama read big thick books and Sharmon decided early on that she wanted to write a book like that herself. She managed to write a few of those, and finished one. She hopes to get back to her fantasy novel-in-progress but enjoys writing poetry, and flash and short fiction so much it may be a while yet.

# A Compilation of Accounts Concerning the Distal Brook Flood

Thomas Ha

The following consists of testimony from the publicly available exhibits filed in *Granger, et al. v. Juna Explorations, LLC.* These transcripts have been excerpted and re-ordered by the Xenobiological Association, but the testimony herein concerning the tragedy of the Distal Brook Flood remains otherwise unaltered.

<u>Excerpt from the Deposition of John Franken – Standard Date 061648</u>

**Q.** Mr. Franken, as you know, my name is Arthur Kim, and I'm one of the attorneys for plaintiffs in this case. I want to thank you for coming in to talk with us today.

**A.** Yes. Of course.

**Q.** Now that we've gone through some of the basics of how the deposition works and talked about your background, I'd like to get into the specific events that brought you here today. Okay?

**A.** Okay.

**Q.** After you finished piloting lunar expeditions for the USS, you said you began work at Juna Explorations, is that correct?

**A.** Yes.

**Q.** And you were stationed on the planet of Ouron, located in the circumstellar habitable zone, or CHZ, of system JE-101, is that correct?

**A.** That's correct.

**Q.** And Ouron is leased by the USS to Juna Explorations for its mining ventures there, correct?

**A.** Yes.

**Q.** And when did you start operating shuttlecraft for the Juna mining colony of Ouron specifically?

**A.** About three and a half years ago.

**Q.** And what were your responsibilities as a pilot on Ouron?

**MR. SRIN:** Objection. Vague.

**A.** Can I... Do I...

**MR. SRIN:** You can answer. The objections are just for the record.

**A.** I'd pilot personnel from Juna facilities to areas off-base.

**Q.** When you say "off-base", you mean you would fly from mining facilities on the body of the gigantiform to other locations on Ouron, correct?

**A.** That's correct. The Juna facilities are concentrated on the organism's hand —two on each finger, two on the thumb, and then one management facility overseeing operations at the wrist.

**Q.** And you would typically pilot flights to and from that management facility, the one on the gigantiform's wrist, correct?

**A.** Yeah, the... Sorry. Most of the locals call it the Sleepy Giant or Giant. But that's right. I would cover the wrist.

**Q.** Understood, Mr. Franken.

I've seen the pictures, and that nickname certainly fits. I can only imagine what an alien organism of that size looks like from above on a shuttlecraft.

**A.** Yeah. It's something... I've come across a lot of things during my time with the USS, but nothing like him—that rocky body, the parts you can see coming out of the planet's surface anyway, stretched out for kilometers like that. Every time I fly over it, I think of the old Earth explorers who wrote about finding God in nature. Those guys would blow their top if they—

**MR. SRIN:** Excuse me, Mr. Franken. I know depositions are unnatural, and you want to treat this like a conversation. But I'd ask that you please wait until Mr. Kim asks you a question. Okay?

**A.** Oh, yeah. Sorry.

**Q.** That's okay, Mr. Franken. I know exactly what you mean.

Now, as you alluded to just now, the way I understand it, the gigantiform is partially submerged in Ouron's surface, but segments of the skull, the hands, parts of the arms, those sit above ground, correct?

**A.** That's correct. Almost like a mountain range. Several kilometers high at some points, depending on where you're at.

**Q.** Okay. And how long would an average flight take, say, from one of the facilities on the gigantiform's hand to the town of Distal Brook?

**A.** Well, Distal Brook was a few kilometers off from the tip of the thumb. Most folks there had some connection to Juna, so they didn't settle too far off. The average flight was maybe an hour, hour and a half, at most.

**Q.** Flight ever take you more than two hours?

**A.** Maybe in bad weather.

**Q.** Ever more than three hours?

**A.** No. Never.

**Q.** And when you're flying a shuttlecraft to or from Distal Brook, you're typically able to see the hand of the gigantiform from up there? Meaning the wrist, thumb, fingers, are all visible to you?

**A.** Yes, that's correct.

**Q.** And I assume you're familiar with Purlicue Lake?

**A.** Yes.

**Q.** Could you describe it for me, please?

**A.** It's the... um... It's the reservoir between the thumb and index finger of the Giant, where the waste from the extraction sites collects until it can be processed.

**Q.** Have you ever been there?

**A.** I only ever visited once and was never in a hurry to get back. The water there is real nasty stuff. Makes you choke and cry your eyes out, just being within a half mile of it.

**Q.** So pretty hazardous, you'd say?

**MR. SRIN:** Objection. Vague and calls for a legal conclusion and/or expert opinion.

**Q.** Withdrawn. Let's switch to something else.

Mr. Franken, you were piloting a shuttlecraft to Distal Brook on Standard Date 022147, correct?

**A.** Yes. I was transporting a Juna Explorations employee from the wrist facility. Don't remember his name though.

**Q.** I'd like to introduce a document that we'll mark as Exhibit 19. If you could take a look at that and let me know when you're done?

**A.** Okay.

**Q.** What is that, Mr. Franken, if you know?

**A.** A flight log for that day, looks like. The passenger listed is a Dr. Mark Granger. Guess that was his name, then.

**Q.** And as far as you know, this log is accurate, correct?

**A.** As far as I know.

**Q.** Do you recall talking to Dr. Granger, that day, when you dropped him off in Distal Brook?

**A.** I think so.

**Q.** What did you two talk about?

**A.** Well, he said he was going to Distal Brook to visit his kid. I remember because our boys were about the same age. He was going to surprise his son for his tenth birthday and—

Sorry. I'm sorry. I've got something in my throat.

**Q.** It's okay. Take your time.

**A.** Sorry. Anyway. He had a kid in Distal Brook, is what I remember.

**Q.** And according to Exhibit 19, you'd already taken off and left Distal Brook when the flood occurred, right?

**A.** That's right.

**Q.** So the day the town flooded, you could see the black water from your shuttlecraft, right?

**A.** I... yeah. I saw the water come down on Distal Brook from the lake. I don't need to tell you it... it took out the whole area at once. Houses and everything. It was like... it was like... God... I don't even know. Just horrible.

**Q.** Understood. I can only imagine, Mr. Franken.

So after the flood hit the town, did you make any stops before heading back to the wrist facility?

**A.** After that? No. I mean, there was nothing I could do. It was all... I mean all wiped out. So I kept going and headed to the wrist facility straight away.

**Q.** Okay, well do you remember a few minutes ago, when you testified that your flight takes about an hour and half, and no more than three hours, and that these logs are accurate as far as you know?

**A.** Yeah, I remember.

**Q.** If you look at the Exhibit 19 again, according to the logs, your return flight from Distal Brook, based on takeoff and arrival, took almost *five* hours.

Why did it take so long, Mr. Franken?

**A.** I... I mean, I don't... I'm not...

**Q.** Did you see something else while you were up there?

**MR. SRIN:** I think now might be a good time for a break. Mr. Kim?

**Q.** Okay. Let's go off the record.

**COURT REPORTER:** Going off the record. The time is 9:37 AM.

<u>Excerpt from the Deposition of Jane Yuan – Standard Date 092949</u>

**Q.** So what was your reason for visiting the colony, Ms. Yuan?

**A.** My brother and his wife had been living there for several years. They kept telling me I should come see them. Spend a couple months and see the Sleepy Giant and all of that.

**Q.** And what were they doing there, your brother and sister-in-law?

**A.** He had a job as an electrician in a Juna facility, which was a dream come true for him. My sister-in-law tagged along on a marriage visa and started working as a teacher at the local elementary.

**Q.** And your brother and sister-in-law lived in the Distal Brook township?

**A.** Yeah. In a small neighborhood called La Roma. They loved it. They really wanted—shit. Sorry. [Inaudible.]

**Q.** It's okay. Take your time. We can take a break if you'd like. Would you like tissues...

**A.** No. I'm fine. [Inaudible.]

Sorry. They wanted to have kids there.

**Q.** Okay. So you were on Ouron on Standard Date 022147, correct?

**A.** Yes.

**Q.** What were you doing that morning?

**A.** My brother and I went hiking at Mammoth Peak. It's a ridge about a couple kilometers away from Distal Brook, where on a clear day you can see the whole hand of the Giant.

Mayra, his wife, had work that day and couldn't join. So my brother and I had breakfast and headed out before sunrise. We wanted to hit the peak before it got too hot, and we were almost there at the top when it happened. The flood.

**Q.** Okay. And what do you remember about the start of the flood, specifically, if you can recall?

**A.** I remember the ground shaking all of a sudden. I know that happened first because I fell over. And right after, there was this sound, like crashing thunder that wouldn't stop.

My brother and I went further up to get a better view, and when we reached the peak, the water was already coming our way. I don't know what I was expecting, but it wasn't that. The water was—it was like this dark wall, ready to crush everything.

**Q.** Do you need to stop?

**A.** No. It's fine.

**Q.** Okay. What happened next?

**A.** It took a few seconds, but we realized the water wasn't going to reach us, that it was going to hit everything in Distal Brook below instead.

Then, when it started happening, the water coming into the town, I remember the other hikers around us all started yelling. And my brother was screaming, I think. This big wall of water, just, it moved past us, and then Distal Brook—all of the buildings, houses, churches, the roofs and walls all broke apart like they were made of paper. I mean, it didn't look real.

The distance we were at, we couldn't see the people. But I mean, you knew. You just knew that they were all getting swept away in there. And it was god awful.

**Q.** And then what happened?

**A.** My brother was losing it for a few minutes, but he calmed down. He got it in his head that Mayra might not have been in the worst of it. He said he saw the water divert around the school where she worked, so it was possible that she or others might try to get on the roof and wait out the currents. So we ran for the car. It took us almost an hour just to get back down the hill.

We drove to the edge of town. But the roads, they were all covered with that black gunk. So we pulled over, waiting for some opening where we might get through. Then others came, people who had been out of the township too. We were all standing at our cars, breathing in the fumes from the water, and I think everyone started bleeding from their noses at some point.

I remember everyone was trying to wipe the blood off their faces.

**Q.** Do you recall any other symptoms of exposure to the black water?

**A.** My eyes were burning at the time. And I started throwing up. Some of my skin, especially around my ankles, the parts that came into contact with the water, peeled off days later.

**Q.** Okay. And do you remember anything else about the flood after that?

**A.** The only other thing was the bodies. I mean, I still don't even know if they were bodies. But these black masses started floating to the surface after a while, like lumps in stew. We tried to pull one out when it got close to us, but we couldn't really touch the water, because of the way it burned.

There was nothing. I mean there was nothing we could do for anyone. We were all just stuck there, waiting, watching the black water carry everything off.

**Q.** And how long were you over there, at the edge of the town?

**A.** A few hours. Until a Juna Explorations team came to lift us out. And we never got to the school, not that it would have made any difference.

**Q.** Where did they take you after that?

**A.** My brother and I spent a couple of months in a facility recovering. Later, some Juna people came and talked to us. They told my brother that they were investigating, but that Mayra, and anyone else still missing, was almost certainly gone.

Then they offered him a settlement. $50,000 and free passage back to Earth. His wife, dead. House, gone. Everyone he knew, drowned. And that was $50,000 to them.

I told him not to sign, but I think after everything he went through, he just wanted it to be over with. To go back home and forget that place ever existed.

**Q.** And did you sign a settlement agreement too?

**A.** No.

**Q.** So after your recovery, you and your brother went back to Earth?

**A.** Yes. I tried to take care of him for a while, but he never really adjusted to being back. And at some point, he joined the TC, and I think it only made him worse.

**Q.** Sorry, TC?

**A.** Titan Church. They're mostly planet-bound, but they're starting to crop up in other systems. They're kind of—what's the word—cultish types, obsessed with the Giant. Anything and everything Giant-related is important to them.

So after the flood, the TC really fixated on the survivors because of their connection to Ouron. They tried to get me to come with them, but I always refused. My brother, though, he didn't have anything else. So he went right along. He attended their masses, and I think he spoke a few times about what he saw on Ouron.

To be honest, I don't really know much more; my brother and I didn't see each other as often once he became a member.

**Q.** I understand, Ms. Yuan. And, I'm sorry to ask. I already know, but I need this for the record. What happened to your brother?

**A.** He passed away late last year. He'd been on a lot of pain medications, because of the black water, and, one day he just, took too much, and... they just found him like that, in his tub. Still not clear if he meant to— Sorry. Just not clear what happened.

Sorry. I don't know what I'm saying any more.

**Q.** It's okay. I just want to say again that I'm very sorry for your loss. And I think this is a good time for a break, but I just want to clarify something.

You're not a party to this lawsuit. You chose to opt out and are here as a third-party fact witness, right?

**A.** Right.

**Q.** So I have to ask. Why not join and sue Juna Explorations like the others?

**A.** No offense, but I don't really see a point. Everything Juna touches is poison, including their money. So fuck them all to hell as far I'm concerned.

**Q.** Okay. Let's take a break.

Excerpt from the Deposition of Teresa De Leon Vol. 1 – Standard Date 020650

**Q.** Okay, Ms. De Leon. Let's look at Exhibit 80 again. That one. The press release regarding your promotion. It says you were elevated to managing director of Ouron on Standard Date 011341, is that right?

**A.** Yes.

**Q.** And it mentions that you started in Juna oversight and management over a decade ago in several colonies before Ouron.

**A.** That's right.

**Q.** And it looks like you pretty much went to work right out of university and have spent your whole career with Juna, correct?

**A.** Yes. That's correct. My predecessor on Ouron, Dr. Oswald, would often say that Juna's purpose was to advance the knowledge of the human species, push us further than we'd ever gone before, and I knew I wanted to be a part of that since I was young.

**Q.** So did you seek a management position on Ouron, specifically?

**A.** Of course.

**Q.** Why?

**A.** Well, in all the decades that the USS has explored other systems, we've only ever encountered a few life forms, most of them microbial. The gigantiform is, to date, the only complex, extraterrestrial organism we've discovered. I don't think there are many people who would pass up the opportunity to help Juna study it.

**Q.** Understood. And in addition to studying the gigantiform, Juna Explorations also extracts resources from it, correct?

**A.** Yes. The gigantiform's body contains a naturally occurring element that has several applications, including as a component in Juna Explorations fuel rods.

**Q.** Cronesium, right?

**A.** Correct.

**Q.** And how is the cronesium extracted? Just the basics, please.

**A.** Because the gigantiform's skin is a type of hardened silicate, it requires several years of drilling. Once we've breached the surface, our engineers use proprietary Juna Explorations tech to scan the surrounding veins and fluid pockets.

After an extraction strategy for the site is determined, we use Oswald derricks to pump the cronesium out of the gigantiform's veins and direct it to a processing facility, where we separate the usable cronesium from other hazardous components in a series of water tanks. From there, the cronesium is directed to another facility, and the waste is ejected.

**Q.** Into Purlicue Lake?

**A.** That's right.

**Q.** And once the waste water is sent to Purlicue Lake, what do you do with it?

**A.** Well. The exact process for neutralizing the waste water is still being worked out. Because it's unstable once the cronesium is removed, we can't reinsert it into the gigantiform or move it elsewhere without great risk.

Juna is on the cusp of a cost-effective method of disposal, but until then it's best stored in the reservoir.

**Q.** And you extract from several facilities on the gigantiform's hand, right? How many Juna Explorations facilities are there on Ouron?

**A.** Eleven.

**Q.** Okay. Thank you. This is all very helpful information, so I appreciate you walking me through it.

Now, to get to more specific issues, you were managing director of Ouron during the events of the Distal Brook Flood, correct?

**A.** Yes.

**Q.** By the way, I should ask, since we may be getting to sensitive territory, did you personally know anyone who was in Distal Brook?

**A.** I did not.

My position as managing director is somewhat solitary.

I rarely leave my post in the wrist facility, so I haven't had the opportunity to visit many of the settlements.

**Q.** Understood. Well, my condolences nonetheless. These were your people, after all, so the loss must not have been easy.

**A.** Thank you.

**Q.** So after the Distal Brook Flood occurred, Juna conducted an internal investigation as to the cause, correct?

**A.** Yes.

**Q.** And if you look at the investigative report previously marked as Exhibit 78 in your stack of documents there. There's a section that's signed by you, Ms. De Leon, right?

**A.** Yes.

**Q.** And it says, "To the best of my knowledge, the results of the foregoing report are a complete and accurate record of the events concerning the Distal Brook township." Do you see that?

**A.** Yes.

**Q.** So you reviewed this and signed off on it, fair to say?

**A.** I did.

**Q.** And above that there's a summary by the investigatory body in that last paragraph, do you see that? If so, can you read that into the record, please?

**A.** It says: "Based on our interviews with relevant personnel and a review of available sensory data, we conclude that the Purlicue Dam spillage was most likely caused by an unanticipated seismic event (U.S.E.), which resulted in an overflow of the Purlicue Dam. Though we recommend construction of additional bulwarks, we believe Juna Explorations took all reasonable and foreseeable measures it could have undertaken to safeguard the hazardous material."

**Q.** And what might cause a seismic event of the kind referred to in that report?

**A.** There are many possible causes. Shift of tectonic plates under the planet surface. Unexpected rupture of a cronesium deposit in the gigantiform's veins. Gas pockets uncovered while drilling.

**Q.** Okay. The report doesn't specify, so I'll ask you. Of those reasons you just listed, what was the cause of the U.S.E. that triggered the flooding of Distal Brook?

**MR. SRIN:** Objection. Calls for speculation.

**A.** Sorry. What?

**Q.** What was the cause of the U.S.E. that triggered the flooding of Distal Brook?

**A.** I'm... Well I wasn't involved in the investigation, so I'm not sure I could speak to that.

**Q.** Okay. But you agreed with this report. So I guess my question is, how did you come to the conclusion that the Distal Brook Flood was caused by a U.S.E.?

**A.** Well, I had no reason to doubt the investigative body.

**Q.** But, to be clear, you reviewed no underlying data to support that finding, did you?

**A.** I did not.

**Q.** Okay. Let's change gears a little bit. Could you look at the photograph in the investigative report, the visual evidence of wreckage in Distal Brook—two pages earlier.

What do you see in the background of that landscape?

**A.** It's... I believe it's the Purlicue Dam...

**Q.** Anything about that look strange to you?

**MR. SRIN:** Objection. Vague.

**A.** I'm not sure what you mean.

**Q.** Do you see any damage to the dam in that picture? Cracks, fissures, anything of that nature?

**A.** It's difficult to know for sure from one photograph. But based on this... I... I mean... No. It doesn't seem to be damaged from what I can see.

**Q.** Now, if the dam had cracked, it'd be a large undertaking to repair it, I assume. You'd have to call in construction teams, halt extraction at nearby facilities, if not do more?

**A.** I... Yes. That's right.

**Q.** And as managing director of Ouron, you'd *know* if something as major as reconstruction of portions of the dam occurred?

**A.** Yes.

**Q.** So to your knowledge, was the dam repaired in that fashion?

**A.** No... not to my knowledge. I believe... the Juna Explorations teams analyzed the damage and told us no further work was necessary.

**Q.** And that didn't seem odd to you?

**MR. SRIN:** Objection. Vague.

**A.** I guess… at the time, there was a lot going on, and I trusted the process.

**Q.** Earlier you were talking about your responsibilities as a managing director. Is safeguarding the health and safety of the colonists one of those responsibilities?

**A.** I'm… yes.

**Q.** And you mentioned that you chose to work on Ouron because you wanted to help humankind, essentially, right?

**MR. SRIN:** Objection. Misstates prior testimony.

**A.** Yes.

**Q.** So if you had the opportunity to protect your fellow man on that colony, you absolutely would have done that, right?

**A.** Yes.

**Q.** But when Juna's off-planet team told you Purlicue Dam didn't need repairs, and didn't identify any specific cause for the flood, you didn't find that strange. Didn't bat an eye, right?

To put it simply, you didn't actually do *anything* to try to figure out what killed all of those people, did you?

**MR. SRIN:** Objection. Kim, this is out of line.

**Q.** Mr. Srin. A question is pending, and Ms. De Leon is in the middle of the answer.

Madame court reporter, read that back, please.

**COURT REPORTER:** To put it simply, you didn't actually do *anything* to try to figure out what killed all of those people, did you?

**A.** I did… I did what I could.

**MR. SRIN:** We're going off the record, right now. Kim. Outside.

**Q.** Thank you, Ms. De Leon. Let's take a short break.

**COURT REPORTER:** And we're off the record.

Excerpt from the Deposition of Charles Bailer – Standard Date 110650

**Q.** Mr. Bailer, did you get any daily reports about activities on Ouron?

**MR. SRIN:** Objection. Vague.

**A.** That *is* vague, isn't it? I don't know if I understand that. Ask it again.

**Q.** Mr. Bailer, did you get any reports about activities on Ouron?

**A.** Well, as CEO, I get a lot of reports. Juna Explorations has over two hundred colonies. Over three thousand research facilities. Over ten million colonist-citizens. So I'm sure I got reports, but it's hard to know what you mean without looking at a specific document.

**Q.** Okay. And do you know what a "U.S.E." is?

**A.** Again, I can't be sure without reviewing documentation. Unanticipated Seismic Event, or something like that.

**Q.** Let's move on to something else. Is the gigantiform dead?

**MR. SRIN:** Objection. Vague. Calls for legal conclusion and/or expert testimony.

**A.** Uh. What?

**Q.** Simple question. Is the gigantiform on Ouron dead? Yes or no.

**MR. SRIN:** Same objections.

**A.** It's an organism that doesn't meet any of the established USS criteria for life. It doesn't metabolize, grow, adapt to its environment, respond to stimuli, or reproduce, as far as we can observe.

**Q.** Is it dead?

**MR. SRIN:** Same objections. And asked and answered.

**A.** Look, it meets no specific criterion for life.

**Q.** Interesting choice of words. Let's take a look at the following, previously marked as Exhibit 49. This is a public document. Take a minute to read it.

**A.** I don't have to. I know it. My father had a copy of this framed in our house.

**Q.** What is the document, Mr. Bailer?

**A.** It's a press statement from Juna's Chief Science Officer, Dr. Malcolm Oswald, from when they announced the discovery of the gigantiform.

**Q.** And Dr. Oswald was also the previous managing director of Ouron, correct?

**A.** That's right.

**Q.** And he established the first extraction facilities and their protocols on Ouron thirty years ago, correct?

**A.** Yeah. You got it. I like this guy. He's very prepared.

**Q.** Thank you, Mr. Bailer. I appreciate your confidence. Now please look at the bottom of the first paragraph. Could you read that into the record, please?

**A.** "This is a remarkable step forward for Juna Explorations and humanity as a whole. Already, this organism has revealed great wonders we have yet to fully understand. Our estimates, judging from the limbs that remain visible on the surface, indicate that its span may be almost 3,000 kilometers, which is larger than most countries and nearly a quarter of the diameter of Ouron itself.

"Based on our silicon dating, we believe the organism is millions of years old, and its positioning and depth in Ouron's crust suggest it may have collided with the planet's surface, quite violently, some time ago, after traveling for some time in the vacuum of space."

**Q.** The rest of that page too, please.

**A.** "The organism appears humanoid, with appendages and an anatomy that suggests it may have, at one point, held itself upright. Though it, interestingly, has no oral cavity or identifiable ocular organs that we've been able to observe.

"Ultimately, however, based on our initial testing, the organism currently meets none of the established USS criteria for active life. It seemingly does not metabolize, grow, adapt to its environment, respond to stimuli, or reproduce. Perhaps the organism did, long ago, function in some way, but either because of its exposure in space or its impact on Ouron, that no longer seems to be the case."

**Q.** What would be different, if the gigantiform were classified as life?

**MR. SRIN:** Same objections.

**A.** We have a whole legal department to figure that out. I'm the wrong person to ask.

**Q.** You might not be allowed, legally, to extract cronesium from the organism at all?

**MR. SRIN:** Same objections.

**A.** Look. I said I don't know. What does this even have to do with this case? Did someone put you up to this? The TC?

**Q.** When you say "TC", are you referring to the Titan Church?

**A.** Who else would I be referring to? Yes. The nutjobs.

**MR. SRIN:** Maybe we should take a break?

**A.** No. It's fine. I just don't like this religious activism invading scientific industry. It isn't right. And you know they're lobbying the Xenobiological Association too. So I can smell them a mile away.

You asking for them or what?

**Q.** Mr. Bailer. I assure you that the only people I represent are the victims of Distal Brook and their families, but let's change topics.

I'm going to mark the following as Exhibit 161. Please take a moment to review.

What is this, Mr. Bailer, if you know?

**A.** It appears to be an annual seismometer output aggregation report for Ouron.

**Q.** And you see that first line, where it says: "Standard Date 112146"? And then next to that it says "U.S.E. registered", right?

**A.** Sure.

**Q.** And, next to that, there's a reference to "B.E. engaged".

What is B.E. a reference to?

**A.** I—I wouldn't know exactly. You'd have to ask the managing director, Ms. De Leon.

**Q.** Okay. As you can see the document goes on with similar dates and U.S.E.s for Standard Year 46, the year prior to the Distal Brook Flood, and by my count there are about one hundred thirty-five U.S.E.s registered, or an average of ten or more, a month.

My question to you is, if these "events" occur with that kind of regularity, how could they possibly be "unanticipated"?

**MR. SRIN:** Objection. Calls for a legal conclusion and/or expert testimony.

**A.** You'd have to ask the seismometer technicians. That's just how we classify them.

**Q.** I'm asking *you*, Mr. Bailer. If there are this many seismic events, at this frequency, your position is that Juna Explorations *doesn't* anticipate them?

**MR. SRIN:** Same objections. And asked and answered. *And* harassing the witness.

**A.** I'm saying, I don't know.

**Q.** But, to your knowledge, no employee of Juna Explorations takes the position that these seismic events can be predicted, right?

**A.** I... I can't speak for every single employee. I don't want to misstate anything.

**Q.** Mr. Bailer. Please stop looking at your attorney. I know Mr. Srin is about to explode in a minute, but he knows full well that you have to answer this question.

I'd also remind you again that you're testifying under penalty of perjury.

Has any Juna Explorations employee, to your knowledge, *ever* asserted that these seismic events can be predicted?

**MR. SRIN:** This is outrageous. I'm dialing the judge's chambers *this second.* Mr. Bailer, please step outside. Counsel, we're going off the record.

**COURT REPORTER:** And we're off the record.

—

**COURT REPORTER:** And we're back on the record.

**Q.** Now that we've stretched our legs and Mr. Srin has gotten that out of his system, let's try this again. Has any Juna employee, to your knowledge, *ever* asserted that these seismic events can be predicted?

**A.** It's possible someone may have.

**Q.** Who?

**A.** Dr. Malcolm Oswald.

**MR. SRIN:** Per our discussion, we're going to designate this portion of the testimony highly confidential pursuant to the stipulated protective order.

[Remainder of testimony redacted.]

<u>Excerpt from the Deposition of Teresa De Leon Vol. 2 – Standard Date 062652</u>

**Q.** Ms. De Leon. Welcome back. It's been some time. Almost a year and a half.

**A.** Yes.

**Q.** I apologize for the delay. It took the attorneys a while to work out a second day of deposition. Nonetheless, we're glad we were able to proceed, as I'm sure you are.

**A.** Yes. I'd just—I'd like this to be done.

**Q.** Before we start, I want to go back to some of your statements in your prior deposition, and we can refer to the transcript if you need it at any point, just let me know. Okay?

**A.** Okay.

**Q.** The last time we spoke, you briefly mentioned the previous managing director on Ouron, Dr. Malcolm Oswald.

How well did you know Dr. Oswald, if at all?

**A.** Reasonably well. He stayed on for a year after I arrived to help with the transition. He taught me everything he knew about the gigantiform, the colony, and his work on Ouron before he returned to Earth.

**Q.** And did you ever keep in contact with him after that?

**A.** Unfortunately, no. He passed away, and we didn't get a chance to connect in the intervening years.

**Q.** Are you aware that after his tenure on Ouron, he began writing publicly about the gigantiform?

**A.** I don't think I heard that... exactly.

I've been told he'd declined a bit in his old age and became a bit troubled, but I'm not aware of the specifics beyond that.

**Q.** Were you aware that, later in life, he disavowed his work as managing director for Juna Explorations and believed that the company had engaged in unethical, abusive practices?

**A.** I... was not. No.

**Q.** Were you aware that his writing gained traction with a number of individuals on Earth, and, after his death, they started an organization dedicated to some of the tenets of his work—an organization known as the Titan Church?

**A.** I've... heard of them. But I'm not sure what this has to do with—

**Q.** Don't worry. We'll discuss that in a moment.

Now, during your last deposition I asked you if you knew anyone in Distal Brook, and you said you did not. Do you recall that discussion?

**A.** Yes.

**Q.** I'd like to introduce the following as Exhibit 284.

What is this, Ms. De Leon?

**A.** It... appears to be a request for leave that I signed for an employee to attend a family event. It's standard for me to do so for certain supervisory positions.

"Child's birthday", it says.

Request came from a... Dr. Mark Granger.

**Q.** Who is Mark Granger?

**A.** He is—I mean he was—a researcher who worked at the wrist facility.

**Q.** Were you close?

**A.** I wouldn't say close, but we knew each other, yes. He was part of a team that tested cronesium applications, so I'd interact with him regularly as part of my duties as managing director.

**Q.** Ever meet his family?

**A.** I... I might have. Maybe a few times for certain special tours. I'd sometimes greet the company families on those occasions. I think I spoke to his wife.

**Q.** How about his kids? Meet his kids?

**MR. SRIN:** Objection. Harassing the witness.

**A.** Two boys, maybe. I'm not sure.

**Q.** And what happened to Dr. Granger, if you know?

**A.** He—excuse me.

He was in Distal Brook at the time of the flood.

**Q.** Meaning he died, correct?

**A.** He—yes.

**Q.** His family too, correct?

**MR. SRIN:** Objection. Harassing the witness!

**A.** Yes.

**Q.** In fact, his older son died on his tenth birthday, the day of the Distal Brook Flood, correct?

**MR. SRIN:** Same objections. What the hell is this, Kim? Are you seriously going to try and—

**Q.** Counsel.

I'm making it clear that we're going to be thorough in correcting the record. I also want to remind Ms. De Leon of her responsibilities as managing director of Ouron before we revisit her other answers.

Now, I've tolerated your interruptions in the past, but I ask that you please refrain from this extensive commentary, which, you know as well as I do, is impermissible during your client's testimony.

**MR. SRIN:** You—

**Q.** I mean it, counsel. Anything beyond simple objections, and I'll be forced to file another motion for sanctions. And you know the judge will be open to granting it again.

Okay.

Now, with that out of the way, please answer the question regarding Dr. Granger's son, Ms. De Leon.

**A.** To my knowledge... Yes. Dr. Granger's son was one of the victims of the flood. His school was... The Distal Brook elementary school was one of the buildings that flooded. A number of colonists, teachers, students were... from what I know... they didn't make it out of the township.

After the last time, the deposition. What you said to me about taking care of the colonists and my responsibilities as a managing director, I—I didn't take that lightly. Really. I took some time to go through the records of people who were in Distal Brook, to get a better sense of who was there. Fathers, mothers, kids, community members. There were... they were all... it was a lot that was lost.

I understand that better now.

And I didn't mean to overlook any of that the last time. Really. I didn't.

Sorry, I don't know what I'm trying to say. And I didn't mean to be overly... emotional about this.

**Q.** Thank you, Ms. De Leon. For what it's worth, I think you're being appropriately emotional, and I appreciate that clarification.

Please set that aside.

Now, the last time you were here, I also asked you how many Juna Explorations facilities were on Ouron. You told me eleven. I assume you were just under stress and overlooked this as well.

I'm going to allow you to correct that statement, right now, if you'd like. I strongly suggest you do.

How many Juna Explorations facilities are on Ouron?

**A.** I...

**Q.** Go ahead, Ms. De Leon.

**A.** Twelve.

**Q.** Thank you. There are eleven extraction facilities on the gigantiform's hand, and then an additional "temple facility" near what we believe to be the organism's skull, correct?

**A.** How do—yes.

**Q.** Thank you.

Now, I told you we'd discuss the Titan Church and its connection to this matter, so let's go back to that.

It turns out, the Church followed Dr. Oswald very closely, and they maintain quite a comprehensive collection of Oswald's personal papers. It makes it convenient to subpoena them, in cases like this, where the opposing party is not always so forthcoming with documentation, and I'd like to share some of that documentation with you now.

Let's enter in the following as Exhibit 300.

What is this diagram, Ms. De Leon?

**A.** It's... it's... Okay. Okay. A moment please.

**Q.** Are you ready to continue?

I'll ask it again.

What is the diagram in Exhibit 300?

**MR. SRIN:** Objection. Document speaks for itself. Calls for specula—

**A.** It's... well—

**MR. SRIN:** —tion.

**A.** It's a draft schematic, showing the designs for a device developed by Juna Exploration for use on Ouron.

We called it the Bitemporal Electrode.

**Q.** And what is the "Bitemporal Electrode"?

Ms. De Leon?

What is the "Bitemporal Electrode"?

**A.** It is a two-part mechanism, drilled and implanted on either side of the gigantiform's skull.

**Q.** And what was the purpose of the Bitemporal Electrode?

**MR. SRIN:** Objection. Vague.

**A.** The device was designed to generate a large amount of energy between the electrodes, which in turn disrupted nearby electrical activity.

**Q.** Meaning, electrical activity in the gigantiform's skull?

**MR. SRIN:** Objection. Misstates prior testimony.

**A.** Yes.

**Q.** If you look at the report previously marked as Exhibit 161, next to indications of U.S.E. events there are concurrent denotations for "B.E. engaged".

Are these recording incidents where the "Bitemporal Electrode" was engaged by Juna personnel?

**MR. SRIN:** Objection. Document speaks for itself—

**A.** Yes.

**Q.** Why did Juna engage the Bitemporal Electrode in these instances?

**MR. SRIN:** Objection. Calls for speculation.

**A.** Whenever we detected the beginnings of a seismic event, usually with an alarm system associated with the seismometers in the wrist facility, we would engage the electrode as a precautionary measure.

**Q.** Why?

**A.** By disrupting electrical activity in the gigantiform, we found that we could often mitigate the seismic activity and lessen the time of the U.S.E.s or halt them altogether.

**Q.** In other words, you'd detect an incoming U.S.E., activate the electrode, and the U.S.E.s would lessen or stop, correct?

**A.** Yes. That's often how it would go.

**Q.** Okay.

In your previous deposition you stated that there were several causes for a seismic event, including tectonic plates shifting, unexpected pockets while drilling, and so on.

Given what you've just told me about the connection between the B.E., the activity in the gigantiform, and the U.S.E.s, is it possible that the gigantiform's body itself is a possible cause for these seismic events?

**MR. SRIN:** Objection. Calls for speculat—

**A.** Possibly. Yes.

**Q.** Could you repeat that?

**A.** Yes. Movement in the gigantiform's body could theoretically be the cause of a U.S.E., though we'd never observed it directly before.

**Q.** Before Distal Brook, you mean?

Strike that. Withdrawn.

Give me a moment.

Do you remember, in your prior deposition, our discussion of photographs of the Purlicue Dam? In particular, the fact that the dam had not been visibly damaged?

**A.** Yes.

**Q.** That's because the dam breaking didn't cause the flooding of Distal Brook, did it?

**MR. SRIN:** Objection. Calls for speculation.

**A.** I... Based on what I know, that does not seem likely. No.

**Q.** Before I get to this next question, I want to remind you of everything we discussed so far and in your prior deposition—the reason you joined Juna, your duties as managing director of the colony, and your relationship with its citizens, including your colleague, Dr. Granger.

With all that in mind, Ms. De Leon, what, based on what you know, could have caused the flooding of Distal Brook?

**MR. SRIN:** Mr. Kim, could we—

**A.** Wait, Mr. Srin. I think I should... I think I do want to answer this.

**MR. SRIN:** Ms. De Leon, I'd really prefer that we discuss this off the—

**A.** Based on the concurrent U.S.E. and the volume of water that cascaded outside the containment area, it's... possible... again I don't know... it's possible that the waste water could have been displaced.

The gigantiform's finger could have shifted, even just slightly, and that would have been enough to trigger the flooding that we observed.

**MR. SRIN:** Objection.

**Q.** What is your objection, Mr. Srin? There's no question pending. Are you objecting to her answer?

**MR. SRIN:** I—withdrawn.

**Q.** Is that what you think happened, the gigantiform's finger shifted?

**A.** I don't... I don't have any direct evidence to confirm that for certain, and, after my last deposition, I spent some time... trying to find records that might give a clearer picture of what occurred.

There is only, to my knowledge, a single flight report from the day of the flood, which references a fault line forming near the gigantiform's index finger. A shuttlecraft pilot radioed for permission to investigate when he was en route to the wrist facility, but the results are heavily redacted except mentions of wreckage in the area—fallen timber that needed to be hauled and service roads to be repaired. I haven't been able to find any more information than that.

Nevertheless, based solely on what I do know about the gigantiform's physiology as well as our facilities and history with the organism... I... I do believe that it's at least... capable of moving as a general matter.

Yes.

**Q.** So, just to be clear, the day the flood occurred, you, as managing director, were at least aware of the *possibility* that the gigantiform could move, correct?

**A.** Again, only theoretically.

But yes. That's correct.

**Q.** And were any of the colonist-citizens of Ouron aware of this theoretical possibility too?

**A.** Not to my knowledge. No.

**Q.** Was your colleague, Dr. Granger, or any of his family, aware of this theoretical possibility?

**A.** I'm— Sorry— Give me a second.

Not to my knowledge... No.

**Q.** And did you, or anyone else in Juna Explorations, take steps to inform anyone on Ouron of the theoretical possibility that the gigantiform could, in fact, move?

**A.** No. We did not.

**Q.** So all of those colonist-citizens who died when that hazardous material overflowed into Distal Brook, they had no idea they were risking their lives, creating a settlement so close to the organism, did they?

**A.** No.

I'm sorry.

**Q.** Why didn't Juna just tell them, any of this? Any of what you're telling me now?

**A.** I... I don't know.

Juna had been mining for decades without incident, and we believed we had an effective mechanism for minimizing any such risk. If... I mean... knowing what I know now, if I could warn them, if I could have foreseen all of this, then I would have.

I just didn't know—

Excuse me.

**Q.** Take your time.

Okay.

Now, whether or not Juna had minimized risk from the gigantiform with the B.E., the organism's movement could potentially indicate that it's still alive, couldn't it?

**A.** It could.

**Q.** And that classification by the USS could complicate Juna Explorations's extraction operations, couldn't it, Ms. De Leon?

**A.** Yes. It could.

**Q.** That could prevent the USS from extracting cronesium, a resource it relies on to produce its fuel rods and that is key to expanding its colonies?

**A.** It… could have that outcome, yes.

**Q.** So it's in Juna's interest to withhold any information that would lead to that outcome, isn't it?

**A.** It would cause problems for Juna if that information were known to others. Yes.

**Q.** Okay.

Okay, Ms. De Leon.

Thank you.

This is… this is a lot of new information we've covered just now, so I'm going to want to go through this again in more detail. It also looks like Mr. Srin is signaling to me that he needs to contact his client, and he and I may have a few more things to discuss as well. But before we go off the record momentarily, I have to ask.

If Juna is suppressing the gigantiform's movement, is it at all possible that the organism is aware of what's happening?

**A.** Aware of what's happening? I don't...

**Q.** That it knows what's going on on Ouron—what Juna is doing to its body, I mean?

**A.** I don't think... I mean there's no way to really know if... I don't know.

**Q.** Never mind.

**A.** Sorry—

**Q.** Forget it.

Withdrawn.

I think that's enough for now.

Let's go off the record please.

**COURT REPORTER:** The time is 11:32 AM, and we are going off the record.

Afterword – JUNA EXPLORATIONS PRESS RELEASE – Standard Date 081652

NEW DISTAL BROOK, Ouron, and NEW YORK CITY, New York—Juna Explorations has reached a $20 billion-dollar, global settlement with the colonists affected by the Distal Brook Flood. The settlement includes dismissal of all current suits concerning or related to the flooding of the Distal Brook township. All other terms of the settlement are confidential.

"Juna Explorations stands behind the brave men and women who comprise our colonies, and we hope that, with this settlement, they, and we, can look toward a safe and secure future among the stars," said Charles Bailer, CEO of Juna Explorations.

"My clients are relieved that they can finally move on with their lives," said lead Plaintiffs' counsel, Arthur Kim. "They believe, and hope, that this tragedy will instruct Juna Explorations operations going forward, so that no one else has to suffer the losses that they have suffered, and no one else will have to endure what they've endured."

Second Afterword- Letter from A. Kim to X.A. Chairman Campos- Standard Date 011254

Dear Chairman Campos,

I'm writing in response to the Xenobiological Association's request for a comment on the "historic victory" achieved by the victims of Distal Brook, as it was phrased in the letter directed to my office. I understand you would like to potentially use any such response as a postscript to a compilation you are preparing concerning the events of the flood. While I cannot discuss the substance of the settlement beyond what is publicly known, I am writing primarily to correct your characterization of the resolution of this case.

As you, and all of the USS, probably know well by now, my clients lost far more than Juna Explorations could compensate them for, and I suspect those who've survived will not know a semblance of peace or normalcy for many years to come. Though the dollar amount presented by Juna Explorations is impressive at a glance, it results in very little for the individual victims once costs are deducted and the settlement is divided by the tens of thousands of plaintiffs, many of whom aren't alive to see that award anyway. The simple truth is that we only accepted the settlement because my clients could not afford, financially or emotionally, to fight the mega-colonies of Juna Explorations in court for another five years. It was for that reason that my firm abstained from collecting its full fees, as did a number of other firms involved in this case.

Meanwhile, mining operations continue on Ouron unchanged. To date, there has been no public analysis or even recognition of the "seismic" risks associated with extraction from the gigantiform. Nor are there any public investigations by the USS that I'm aware of into the classification of the gigantiform as a non-living entity.

The organization known as the Titan Church has filed for various injunctions, but those suits have yet to go anywhere as of the writing of this letter. So, for all intents and purposes, everything on the colony remains the same as it did six years ago, barring the absence of one small town and everything it once contained.

You asked for a response to include in your compilation regarding our victory, but the only response I have for you is this:

"What victory?"

Sincerely,

Arthur Kim

*See Thomas Ha's story "A Compilation of Accounts Concerning the Distal Brook Flood" online at Metaphorosis.*
*If you liked it, leave a comment. Authors love that!*
*Remember to subscribe to our e-mail updates so you'll know when new stories are posted.*

## About the story

I was a lawyer in another life, and I always found it funny in legal dramas when some major revelation resolved a case decisively and tidily. While I wouldn't claim the legal mechanics of this particular story are realistic, I wanted to write something that captured more of the anti-climactic reality of most cases (albeit in a grander, sci-fi setting), which is that, even if cases do uncover something substantial, they usually just settle, often to the benefit of the more powerful party and without much disturbance to the status quo. As for the ecological disaster described in the story itself, it's loosely based on coal slurry floods, which are unfortunately a real byproduct of the mining industry and have catastrophic effects on communities and surrounding environments.

## A question for the author

Q: What kind of pieces are the most fun to write?

**A:** I tend to enjoy writing slower, contemplative pieces. I like faster-paced action too; I just don't think I've ever been able to write it believably.

## About the author

Thomas Ha is a former attorney turned stay-at-home father who enjoys writing speculative fiction during the rare moments when both of his kids are napping at the same time. Thomas grew up in Honolulu and, after a decade plus of living in the northeast, now resides in Los Angeles.

www.thomashawrites.com, @ThomasHaWrites

# Copyright

## Title information

Metaphorosis April 2021

ISSN: 2573-136X (online)
ISBN: 978-1-64076-197-1 (e-book)
ISBN: 978-1-64076-198-8 (paperback)

## Copyright

## Works of fiction

This book contains works of fiction. Characters, dialogue, places, organizations, incidents, and events portrayed in the works are fictional and are products of the author's imagination or used fictitiously. Any resemblance to actual persons, places, organizations, or events is coincidental.

## All rights reserved



## Moral rights asserted

Each author whose work is included in this book has asserted their moral rights, including the right to be identified as the author of their respective work(s).

## Publisher

Metaphorosis

a magazine of speculative fiction

Metaphorosis Magazine is an imprint of
Metaphorosis Publishing
Neskowin, OR, USA

www.metaphorosis.com

"Metaphorosis" is a registered trademark.

## Discounts available

Substantial discounts are available for educational institutions, including writing workshops. Discounts are also available for quantity purchases. For details, contact Metaphorosis at metaphorosis.com/about

# Metaphorosis Publishing

Metaphorosis offers beautifully written science fiction and fantasy. Our imprints include:

Metaphorosis Magazine
Plant Based Press
Verdage

You can also find us:
@MetaphorosisMag, @MetaphorosisRev, @Metaphorosis
www.facebook.com/metaphorosis

Help keep Metaphorosis running by supporting us at
Patreon.com/metaphorosis

See more about some of our books on the following pages.

# Metaphorosis Magazine

Metaphorosis is an online speculative fiction magazine dedicated to quality writing. We publish an original story every week, along with author bios, interviews, and notes on story origins.

We also publish monthly print and e-book issues, as well as yearly Best of and Complete anthologies.

Come and see us online at magazine.Metaphorosis.com

## Metaphorosis:
## Best of 2020

The best science fiction and fantasy stories from *Metaphorosis* magazine's fifth year.

## Metaphorosis
## 2020

*All* the stories from *Metaphorosis* magazine's fifth year. Fifty-two great SFF stories.

## Metaphorosis: Best of 2019

The best science fiction and fantasy stories from *Metaphorosis* magazine's fourth year.

## Metaphorosis 2019

*All* the stories from *Metaphorosis* magazine's fourth year. Fifty-two great SFF stories.

### Metaphorosis:
### Best of 2018

The best science fiction and fantasy stories from *Metaphorosis* magazine's third year.

### Metaphorosis
### 2018

*All* the stories from *Metaphorosis* magazine's third year. Fifty-two great SFF stories.

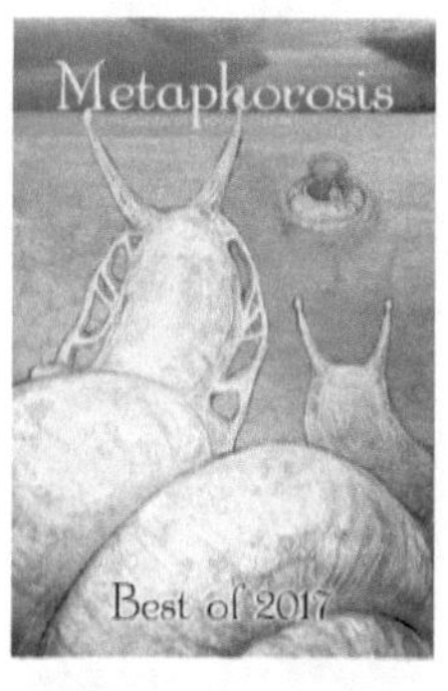

## Metaphorosis:
## Best of 2017

The best science fiction and fantasy stories from *Metaphorosis* magazine's *second* year.

## Metaphorosis
## 2017

*All* the stories from *Metaphorosis* magazine's second year. Fifty-three great SFF stories.

## Metaphorosis:
## Best of 2016

The best science fiction and fantasy stories from *Metaphorosis* magazine's first year.

## Metaphorosis
## 2016

*Almost* all the stories from *Metaphorosis* magazine's first year.

# Plant Based Press

Vegan-friendly science fiction and fantasy, including an annual anthology of the year's best SFF stories.

### Best Vegan SFF of 2020

The best vegan-friendly science fiction and fantasy stories of 2020!

### Best Vegan SFF of 2019

The best vegan-friendly science fiction and fantasy stories of 2019!

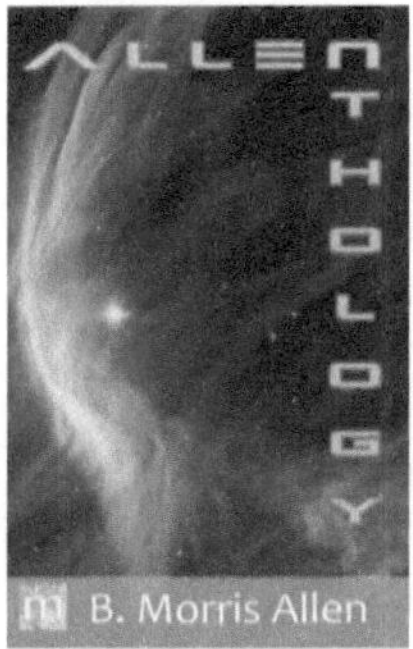


## Susurrus

A darkly romantic story of magic, love, and suffering.

## Allenthology: Volume I

A quarter century of SFF, including the full contents of the collections *Tocsin, Start with Stones,* and *Metaphorosis.*

# Verdage

---

*Verdage*

Science fiction and fantasy books for writers – full of great stories, often with an additional focus on the craft of speculative fiction writing.

### Reading 5X5 x2

*Duets*

How do authors' voices change when they collaborate?

A round-robin of five talented science fiction and fantasy authors collaborating with each other and writing solo.

Including stories by Evan Marcroft, David Gallay, J. Tynan Burke, L'Erin Ogle, and Douglas Anstruther.

# Score

*an SFF symphony*

What if stories were written like music? *Score* is an anthology of varied stories arranged to follow an emotional score from the heights of joy to the depths of despair – but always with a little hope shining through.

## Reading 5X5

*Five stories, five times*

Twenty-five SFF authors, five base stories, five versions of each – see how different writers take on the same material.

## Reading 5X5

*Writers' Edition*

Two extra stories, the story seed, and authors' notes on writing. Over 100 pages of additional material specifically aimed at writers.